Ways to Spend the Night

WAYS TO SPEND THE NIGHT

STORIES

Pamela Painter

Engine Books
Indianapolis

Engine Books
PO Box 44167
Indianapolis, IN 46244
enginebooks.org

Also available in eBook formats from Engine Books.

Printed in the United States of America

10   9   8   7   6   5   4   3   2   1

ISBN: 978-1-938126-35-2

Library of Congress Control Number: 2015953371

Contents

Reading in His Wake

"AT LAST," MY HUSBAND said, when I had closed the curtains for the night and come to bed.

"You knew I would," I said.

"But I didn't know when." Propped up in the rented hospital bed, he peered more closely at my chosen book. A novel by Patrick O'Brian. "Wait, no, no," he said. "You must begin at the beginning."

"But I like the sound of this one," I said, drawing out the swish of *The Mauritius Command.*

"But you want to be there when Aubrey and Maturin meet."

"I can always go back," I said, only slightly petulant, aware that at another time I would have been reading favorites, Trevor, Atwood, or Munro. Or tapping into the wall of biographies across from our beds, Marshall's *The Peabody Sisters*, or Ellman's *Joyce.* Continuing through the poetry at the top of the stairs: Rivard, Roethke, Ruefle, Solomon, Szymborska. We'd never see that time again.

His eyes gleamed. "But Aubrey and Maturin meet at such an unlikely place—especially to begin the series. A concert. Italians on little gilt chairs playing Locatelli." He stopped, out of breath. "Never mind."

"So what's the first one?" If I was going to do this, give him this gift, so to speak, I would do it right. He named *Master and Commander* and, ignoring the irony, I did as commanded and retrieved *Master and Commander* from his study next door. Carefully I settled in beside him, our old queen set flush to his new bed, and embarked. In running commentary over years of hurried breakfasts and long dinners, he'd extolled to me Patrick O'Brian's sheer genius: how in the first novel he delivers to the reader in dramatic scenes of tense negotiation a detailed account of everything that Jack Aubrey must buy to outfit a ship circa 1859.

Four pages and an introduction later, I said, "I see what you mean. A most prickly meeting. Maturin delightfully pissy because a rapt Aubrey, from his seat in the scraggly audience, is audibly 'conducting' the quartet a half beat ahead."

"Don't forget their terse exchange of addresses as if for a duel," he said, laughing and coughing. I looked toward the oxygen machine, then at him. He shook his head.

Relieved, I slid the damp shoulder of his nightshirt into place. "Conflict on page one," I said, making us both happy.

Fifty pages later, when I murmured "mmmmmm," he said "what? Tell me." He turned on the pillow with effort and put aside his own O'Brian, *The Truelove.* So I read for him "...the sun popped up from behind St. Philip's fort—it did, in fact, pop up, flattened sideways like a lemon in the morning haze and drawing its bottom free of the land with a distinct jerk."

" '...distinct jerk,'" he repeated.

I said again "...drawing its bottom free of the land with a distinct jerk." A shared blanket of satisfaction settled over us and we went back to our books, companionably together, and companionably apart.

When I stopped reading to bring him a fresh glass of water to chase his myriad pills, he wanted to know where I was now. I slipped back into bed and tented the book on my flannel chest as I described how Mowett, an earnest member of the square-rigged ship's crew, is explaining sails to a queasy Maturin, and here my husband smiled wryly in queasy recognition of feeling queasy. I took his hand, and went on to describe how Maturin affects interest, although he is exceedingly dismayed to receive this lesson at the appalling height of forty feet above the roiling seas. "Meanwhile, the reader is getting the lesson too—and drama at the same time. Here," and I read, "The rail passed slowly under Stephen's downward gaze—to be followed by the sea...his grip on the ratlines tightened with cataleptic strength."

"It makes me want to start all over again," my husband said. Then, not to be seen as sentimental, he held up his book to show he'd just finished. It slipped to the rug and we left it there.

"You could read Dave Barry now," I said, acknowledging the only good thing about our new sleeping arrangement. My husband used to read Barry's essays in bed, laughing so hard the bed would shake, shaking me loose from whatever I was reading. Annoyed, I'd mark my page and say, "OK, read it to me." The ensuing excerpt was a tone change and mood swing one too many times—I finally banished Dave Barry from the bed after a column had my husband out of bed and pacing with laughter. In it, Dave Barry refers to an article published in a Scottish Medical journal, "The Collapse of Toilets in Glasgow." Barry says, "The article describes the collapsing-toilet incidents in clinical scientific terminology, which contrasts nicely with a close-up, full-face photograph, suitable for framing, of a hairy and hefty victim's naked wounded butt, mooning out of the page at you, causing you to think, for reasons you cannot explain, of Pat Buchanan." We said it again and again. It answered everything: "for reasons you cannot explain."

"Do you want a Dave Barry book?" I asked. He didn't answer. He was either sleeping or wishing I would shut up.

When we were about to leave for radiation, he was still bereft of a new O'Brian. I found him standing in his study, leaning on a walking stick from his collection, now no longer an affectation.

"The "W's" are too high," he said, stabbing the air with his stick. "It's Wodehouse I'm after."

"Why Wodehouse?" I said. Jeeves, the perfect valet and gentleman's gentleman, would be totally disapproving of my husband's un-ironed shirts and his trousers drooping on his thinning hips. "I'm almost finished with Trevor's *After Rain*, it has that startlingly dark story about…"

"I think I'll read Wodehouse," he said, his jaw set. Out of breath, he slumped into his desk chair and pointed again, "But I can't reach him." On the shelves behind where my husband was pointing ranged the two hundred plus books he'd edited at a Boston publishing house, and the four he'd written, the last novel, *A Secret History of Time to Come,* included by the New York Museum of Natural History in a time capsule that would outlast us all. "We have too many books," he said.

"That's what you always say," I said. Hitching up my skirt before the wall of English and European fiction, I mounted the wobbly wooden ladder we swore at on principle every time we retrieved an out-of-reach book. Waugh, Winterson, Wodehouse. I called down three titles before he nodded at the fourth. *The Code of the Woosters.*

"Why Wodehouse," I asked again on my descent.

"Ah, you haven't read Wodehouse yet. Arch, mannered humor. You'll see." Then, as if anticipating my early mutiny against O'Brian in deference to Wodehouse, his eyes narrowed, and he instructed, "Keep with the O'Brians for now."

We left for the hospital, armed with our respective books. On the way, I mentioned that Raymond Chandler, also English, and Wodehouse had both attended the posh prep school, Dulwich College. " 'Dul-ich' but spelled Dulwich," my husband said, surprised by Chandler.

Our bookish, competent doctor always wanted to know what we were reading. My husband waved the Wodehouse at him. "It has a blurb by Ogden Nash," he said, and read, "In my salad days, I thought that P.G. Wodehouse was the funniest writer in the world. Now I have reached the after-dinner coffee stage and I know that he is."

"Woadhouse," the doctor said, making a note on his prescription pad.

"W-o-o-d. I hope he's still funny," my husband said, peering at the doctor over his glasses. "I'm way past the after-dinner coffee. I've reached the medicine stage."

A week later, we were again side by side, my husband's bed rising smoothly and electronically to a barely comfortable position I tried to match with pillows, despairing of the difference in height. I'd finished *Master and Commander* and put it in a safe place because the doctor had meticulously written his home phone number inside its cover. *Post Captain* was next. My husband's long fingers, thin and bony, were oddly free of books. He was listening to the tape of O'Brian's latest Aubrey/Maturin, *The Wine-Dark Sea*. His eyes were alertly closed beneath the Walkman's earphones curving over his new, silky growth of hair.

When he stopped listening to take his pills, I asked him to recall what he'd liked best about *Post Captain*. I closed my eyes against a hysterical welling up of water. And when he'd told me, I thought yes, yes, after years of reading and rereading, arguing, damning and praising, I knew now almost exactly what he would say. I didn't tell him this—but tested more. I badgered him about the repetition of one battle scene after another, asked him to name his favorite title in the series, asked him if Maturin ever dies. I moved on to Ford's *The Good Soldier*, didn't the narrator's equivocation grate on his nerves? Yes and no. Who was Dante's best translator? Yes, yes. And what did he think of the poem in *Pale Fire*?

"Stop it," he said, his voice stronger than it had been in days. "Enough."

The next evening, when he had finished both sides of the first tape, he told me to look in his desk for a second Walkman. Why didn't matter. "Now, listen to this tape," he said.

"You're still seducing me with literature," I accused him.

He took the tape from his Walkman and inserted it into mine.

"No. No. I can't," I said. "I'll get the plots mixed up." Already I was awash in the unfamiliar world of sloops and frigates, admiring of royals, baffled by masts and yards, and dipping in and out of *A Sea of Words: A Lexicon and Companion for Patrick O'Brian's Seafaring Tales*, chastely beside me on the bed. In love again.

"Here," he said. "Listen."

I donned the earphones and because he was watching I closed my eyes. Across the tiny gulf between our beds, his hand found my hand as a calming voice began, "A purple ocean, vast under the sky and devoid of all visible life apart from two minute ships racing across its immensity…"

Until my husband's hand slipped from mine, until his breath failed, until I called 911, until the ambulance arrived to provide our last voyage together, on that last evening I sailed precariously in two different seas, astride two listing vessels, keeping a third in view against a dark horizon, reading in his wake.

Fenced In; Fenced Out

ALL WEEK, BELLE'S HUSBAND, Streak, had been setting fences at Joey's cousin's funeral home in Hot Springs, prepared at any moment to halt the job and put things to rights if some bereaved family was in sudden need of the Setzer Funeral Home's services. To avoid commuting three hours back and forth, Streak and Joey stayed nights in a motel Streak called Pass-the-Night. They started early and worked late to get the job done. Streak called home twice and both times he and Belle had argued over the accounting course Belle was taking at night school, Streak still mad about the week before when she wouldn't leave class early for the bowling banquet at the Elks. He'd skulked outside her classroom and later had the gall to suggest she might be getting some extra tutoring when he was out of town. She said where on earth did he get such ideas—even if Mr. Brace was young and handsome, which he wasn't; he was fat, smart, and married.

Friday, when Streak came home, he started up again about Belle's accounting class while she was sorting his week's laundry into darks and lights.

"You're the only one who's messed up our books so far," she told him, meanly satisfied to bring it up if he was going to revisit that issue. "That woman last year bought herself a fence and thought you ended up on her side of it." A million times she'd pictured the woman standing on her porch in a fuzzy housecoat watching Streak work, changing into something thin and frilly to ask him to move her piano or listen to her furnace. Belle found out by chance when a broken gas line on Main Street and a long detour took her past the woman's newly-fenced-in

13

yard, Streak's truck in the drive when he should have been at the new job on the other side of town. She'd rung the woman's doorbell long and hard, then lifted and let fall a hefty pot of geraniums on the woman's porch. She waited in her car till they came to the door minutes—too many minutes—later, and then she'd peeled away.

"That's all behind us," Streak said, tugging a pale blue workshirt out of her hands, and wrapping them both in its soft, sour smell. He was right, and besides, it hurt to remember, so she stopped, but everything painful has its own ghost.

Later that evening, the washing machine still churning, Belle was half watching the Dodgers game go into extra innings and doing accounting homework. Streak, all attention on the game, was holding a cold beer to his forehead. That's when she noticed his wedding ring was missing. His ring matched hers, etched gold bands with tiny cut-out hearts they'd traveled to Hot Springs to buy. Her mother had disapproved of the double-ring ceremony. "A ring on a man's finger is just an excuse for him to take it off," she'd warned. Even when Belle's ring was solid with detergent after cleaning up at McClard's Barbecue, she didn't take it off, but scrubbed it with an old toothbrush she kept at work for just that purpose. "Where's your wedding ring?" she asked.

"I'll get another ring," Streak said, his eyes on the game.

"It wouldn't be the same," she said. "But where's the one you had? You lost it?"

"Well, I wouldn't say it's lost," he said. "It's there somewhere."

"There? Where?"

"In Hot Springs."

"Was there a woman involved?" she asked, already seeing her—a bleached blonde, red lipstick filling out thin lips, tight black pants.

Streak pulled her over to him saying, "You're crazy. It's just you and me, Belle."

She buried her nose in the fencing of his ribs, her voice muffled and still needing to know. "If you didn't lose it, what did you do with it?" She pictured him at work all week in Hot Springs, bare-chested and sweating, a red bandana tied around his forehead and another in his pocket. His hands would be red, the calluses surrounded by blisters from holding the new electric post digger still and tight. He'd probably tucked the ring in his pocket and sometime later along that hot row of new fence he'd pulled out the dry bandana and sent the ring flying. That night, while showering at the motel, he'd miss it but be too tired to go back for a look, and still pissed about her night school. She nudged him. "Well?" She could feel him staring intently at the Dodgers' catcher, guessing at the signals to the pitcher. And avoiding hers.

He squeezed her shoulder. "What do you think he's going to call for? A curveball? Maybe a slider?" He'd once told her she knew more about baseball than his coach. "Come on. What's he going to throw?"

"I don't know," Belle said, her face still buried in his ribs. "Maybe a curveball so fast his ring goes with it and makes a one-inch dent in the catcher's glove."

He sighed. "It's more like I got mad and left it behind."

"Why mad? Behind where?"

"I told you. In Hot Springs." He handed her the beer and she took a slow, thoughtful drink. Now she pictured him inside the kitchen of Joey's cousin's funeral home, getting a glass of ice water mid-morning or a beer mid-afternoon. His hands would be cramping and he'd ease off the ring, rub his sore fingers across his bare chest for moisture in a gesture that made her knees weak. He'd set the ring down and like the look of it there on the table. He'd make some feeble joke about her moving up in the world with night classes and Joey would probably shrug and say everyone has problems. Joey's cousin probably is keeping it on the windowsill for the next time he sees Joey.

"So you can get it back," she said. Streak thought about it while the pitcher hung low, waiting for the catcher's sign, and easily struck the batter out, and then he said sure, he wanted it back, too. Tomorrow they'd take a trip to Hot Springs.

In the morning when they could have been painting the back porch railing or buying beer from that new microbrewery for Saturday night poker, they were getting gas on their way out of town.

As Streak threw a new spare into the back of the pickup, she could tell that he was feeling a little sheepish by the way he nodded to Billy, avoiding small talk, telling him to put it on their account. Billy used to catch for Streak on the high school team and like most people in town he still called Daniel "Streak." In their senior year, Streak had been the school hero, taking the team all the way to state. His mother wasn't impressed by all the fuss. "Gallons of milk filling the fridge, the grass going wild, squealing girls calling at all hours," his mother complained to Belle. "Their cars parading by the house. He doesn't know what to make of it. Thank heavens he's going steady with you." His mother never knew they broke up for a few months when Streak noticed one of those girls, a pert cheerleader bent on winning him. Now, at twenty-seven, Streak was still tall and lean, skinned down to muscle and bone with hair the color of light molasses. But Belle knew they all still pictured him, herself included, in tight baseball knickers, his hand drooping behind him with the weight of the ball, the oiled glove held tight to his chest, as he squints at Billy's signal for the next pitch.

"See you at poker night," Billy said, slapping their fender.

Maybe, Belle thought.

First they stopped at McClard's for bacon, grits, and eggs. Patty brought them two full plates without asking. Since the Cedar plant lay-offs last year, Saturdays were slow except for people hauling in their meat to be smoked. Belle always arrived home reeking of barbecue. She'd throw her clothes out on the back porch till there was enough for a separate wash. Streak liked that smell, but it was one of the reasons she needed to change jobs. This morning she was wearing a slim skirt and sleeveless crisp blouse, the way she hoped to dress for work someday soon. Dresses with matching belts, high heels. Trouble was men didn't keep up. You saw couples, the woman in a dressy skirt and blouse and heels, and her guy in an old varsity jacket or windbreaker with a bowling insignia on the back, pulling on a baseball hat, holding the back in place with one hand, tugging down the brim with the other. Though Belle had to admit she enjoyed seeing Streak's hands employed this way—his sharp, jutting elbows and tucked-in chin.

Streak doused his eggs with A1 as Patty came by with refills of coffee. She asked where they were headed and Belle said Hot Springs to look around. Uncanny how people could tell you were leaving town before you left. She told Patty she'd see her Monday and tucked a ten dollar bill under her mug. Big tippers were girls who'd worked behind counters in those very same shoes.

A bright sun on a clear day always brought on the sky's deepest shade of blue, made darker by Belle's glasses. She had a few brief moments of doubt, of wondering if the trip was worth it, but she was superstitious enough to need Streak to wear the real ring from their wedding. He drove with his elbow out the window, his left hand playing the steering wheel. If he'd been wearing his ring it would have been pinging against the wheel to bluegrass like it must have been when he and Joey headed out. She wondered what their motel was like, maybe a fancy place that Joey's cousin got them cheap. In-ground pool. Streak said she'd have liked the massage bed. Maybe they wouldn't rush home tonight. She pictured them strolling around in one of the glittering new malls, reading menus to decide where to eat, holding hands through a first-run movie. Later, they would lie in bed with the air-conditioning on blast, squandering quarters they'd have stacked on the bedside table, ready to feed the massage bed vibrating beneath them after making hot, slow love. She'd wait and see what they found and where they found it.

The day heated up, making her drowsy, so she slouched down to ride with her long hair whipping out the window, wishing she had her books to study. She liked accounting, its system of checks and balances, columns of numbers, making things even on both sides of the ledger, then seeing what's left. It could take forever to resolve an eight cent error. But accounting was something she'd always done. Streak was a man of few words, so she'd gotten used to accounting for his day from the sketchiest of details. "So their check probably bounced," she'd say. Or "I'll bet Joey left you to finish up again." Or "That means you'll be working through the weekend so I better trade poker night with Jace and Sally." He was never surprised. He probably thought he told her these things.

Today, Streak surprised her by talking more than usual. As they wound through the small towns he preferred to the state highway, his eyes scanned the houses on either side of the road. "See there," he said, and pointed to a house with an undefended garden, "And there." He nodded toward another house with a swing set planted much too close to the road. Caring that he cared, she reached to put her hand on his tense leg, and he briefly covered it with his. "Poor mutt," he said, nodding to a scrawny, limp dog tied to a tree. "Their owners are too cheap to put up a fence but they can buy a satellite dish the size of a garage." Most people, he said, were clueless about their property lines, too. They'd sign a contract and shell out a down-payment and sure'n hell as soon as he and Joey began work the neighbor would come steaming out to dispute where the new fence was going. They'd have to stop work until a surveyor came on the scene to settle things. Half the time the fence got pulled up and moved, sometimes only two inches. "Every fence we put in, we ask 'You sure you know your property boundaries?' and sure, they're sure. It's the neighbors who aren't." He looked over at her.

"Why don't you go to school for surveying?" she said. It's what he'd planned on doing once he didn't make it into the minors. A torn muscle had put an end to that.

"We're required by law to stop work the minute trouble starts," he said. "It's hell on the schedule. And stockade is the only fence that picks up and moves well."

Stockade was Streak's favorite. He'd been saving stockade extras in the back of the garage for when they had a need—vegetables, dogs, kids. They'd decided to wait on kids till she had a job that took her out of McClard's and set her behind a desk in an insurance office or bank where she could save up for later. She closed her eyes, content to listen to Streak install more strangers' fences.

When they got to Hot Springs, he drove straight to Joey's cousin's funeral home, but only, it turned out, to show her the neat white picket fence. They pulled up to the curb, and she had expected him to hop out and go knock on the back door, explain about the lost ring, but he just sat there admiring his work.

"No one died, so we finished in record time. That was the deal."
She was brushing the tangles from her hair as a black hearse pulled
up beside them and into the driveway. Streak nodded discretely at the
driver who nodded discretely back and pulled the hearse around to the
unloading bay.

"Where we going now?" she asked.

"You'll see," Streak said and soon they were headed out the other
side of town, past bars and muffler shops and cheap motels. Signs
everywhere advertised the healing powers of the hot springs that ran
hot even during winter, a miracle in itself.

Finally they slowed down at the entrance to a pink and gray motel
that really was called Pass-the-Night. Belle felt oddly disappointed;
she thought he'd made it up.

"This is it," Streak said. "Room Ten."

Ten was on the ground floor of a long, two-story building. The
parking space in front was empty, so they slid in. She was surprised
the ring was here, having pictured it nearer the funeral home's new
fence. Now she saw Streak hunched over on the side of a sagging bed,
the phone held hard in the curve of his shoulder as he tugged off his
steel-toed boots and complained about her night school. She'd finally
hung up on him. And now she imagined him twisting off his ring and
plunking it down next to a Gideon bible on the rickety bedside table
without a drawer, knocking it to the floor in his sleep.

Holding her hair back, she peered in Ten's dusty window. Streak
would have to be the one to crawl around on some stained carpeting or
grainy linoleum, feel under the dresser, the TV stand and bed.

"This isn't where I threw the ring," he said, behind her.

Threw was new.

She turned to study him, his hands jammed into his back pockets,
his legs spread wide to black boots. His jaw was set in a silence his
mother lamented in his father, among other attributes, so Belle looked
out past the pickup to consider the entire asphalt parking lot, a gray
outfield in an older game. This time she saw him slamming down the
phone and going to the door to let in the cooler night air, leaning against

the jamb as he finished off a six-pack. Probably he'd been wishing he'd gone along with Joey-the-happy-bachelor to the bars down the way, flirting with girls, acting like he'd just pitched a no-hitter. Envious of Joey's night, he'd have ripped off his ring and thrown it past the truck, listened for the sound of it hitting the flickering neon sign.

Belle headed out in that direction. Streak called her back. She couldn't read his eyes under the brim of his baseball hat. "I think it's on the roof," he said, hitching his thumb toward the room on top of Room Ten.

She squinted up at the hot flat line of the motel roof, two stories up and no doubt scalding. Heat would be rising in cartoon squiggles from black tar patches.

"We'll have to find a way up there," Streak said. He peered down the length of the motel, hoping to avoid the dinky office, she could tell. *Vacancy* was an understatement.

The office was crawling with lovingly tended spider plants. An old man with leathery skin and thick white hair was tuned into a hospital soap as if waiting for his own diagnosis. He said his daughter was gone for the day, but he found their request interesting enough to peer at them before pointing to a rusted metal door behind the counter that led to the heat and air-conditioning systems, and also the stairs to the roof. "Never been up there myself," he added, his curiosity draining away.

The cement stairs smelled like a crypt beneath a hatch door that grated as Streak lifted it and laid it back. He reached down to pull Belle up over the tar-paper lip, but she ignored his hand and climbed through onto a patchy sheet of blinding white gravel. Puddles of black tar floated and burned.

You threw your ring up here," she said. "From down below."

"From over there." Streak pointed to a '78 Mustang under the Pass-the-Night sign.

"What were you doing way out there?"

"Well, I'd had a lot to drink," Streak said. His head bent low, he was already into the search, diligently scuffing the gravel with the toe of one boot and then the other.

"You know Joey," he said. "Always bragging about my pitching."

"Bragging? Who was Joey bragging to?"

Streak's head came up for a brief moment as if to see who, too, and then he went back to scuffing gravel like he used to do on a pitcher's mound. "Oh, two girls he met one night when he went out for a beer. You know Joey's stories about my fastball."

Belle put her glasses on. She didn't need to hear more. She knew what happened to Streak's ring. After she hung up on him, Streak would have slammed down the phone and gone to Joey's room to see if he'd left yet. Joey would be putting the finishing touches on his wet hair, glad to have Streak's company. "Like old times," Joey probably said. Joey would have talked about a new job while Streak tucked his wallet into his back pocket, sorted quarters for the jukebox from change meant for the solitary bed massage.

They probably bar-hopped till they found what they were looking for: someone who remembered "The Streak" from local headlines about their loss, his big win. Girls whose brothers or cousins or boyfriends had been defeated by Streak's pitching. Joey would have gone into his spiel, telling old high school stories that beat installing fences any day. At last call, he'd suggest that maybe Streak could do a demonstration of the pitch that had been clocked at 101. Giggling, the girls would have followed Joey's pickup back to Pass-the-Night where Streak would toss a few stones in the parking lot, aiming at a lamp pole or dumpster. "Hey, we have more cold beer inside," Joey would say. "Aren't you married," one of the girls might have said to Streak, coyly and briefly playing fair. "Here's what I think of that," Streak would have said, twisting off the gold wedding band, ignoring the ridges of the tiny cut-out hearts. Then, his leg taut and high in the pitcher's wind-up, in the movement every woman loved, straining the seams of his jeans, his shirttail flapping, he would have thrown the ring. The prettiest girl, understood to be his, would clap softly. But he'd be listening to hear the ring arc silently up and over the motel roof. Streak alone would have heard the tinny failure of his pitch—metal on gravel—as the others applauded with whistles and shushes and nudges and Joey again issued an invitation the girls could not resist.

Seeing that she knew, he said, "It just seemed to happen." He was peering out over the back lots of bars and body shops, not a fence in sight.

"That's what you said last time," she said.

"It didn't mean anything."

He'd said this before too. It was something she could decide to trust—if she wanted to. Even confused, she understood the coiled force of his body, the heat and anger and longing in his throw. The possibility of extra innings in a close hard game. She could almost feel the girl's laughter vibrating in her own throat, the wind ruffling her own long hair, as if, just this moment, his ring was sailing up toward her under a full indulgent moon to land precisely, softly at her feet. Which is why, seconds later, when she found his ring she kept it. The beginning of the end, and that, too, she kept to herself.

Last Weekend

ALL OF THE GUESTS broke something; it was that kind of weekend. Furthermore, Ilene suspected that the Wests, who had broken her Melior coffeepot, would somehow not feel obliged to replace it after they heard that she and Mark were getting a divorce. The issue of the ruined pot would get lost in their protests of surprise or dismay—and silent, hoped-for immunity.

She had studied how people break the news of a divorce, which she and Mark had considered a year ago in answer to his infidelities and her acquired indifference. Then one night, as Ilene lay in bed reading, Mark came upstairs to say he had called his parents. His eyes were bloodshot from weeping and for the first time, Ilene imagined the call to her own parents, saw the frozen, scared faces of Molly, nine, and Stevie, seven, as she and Mark rearranged their lives. "We can't do it to them," she said.

But their reconciliation had merely delayed the inevitable one more year: a year filled with old whispered arguments and accusations while the children listened from the stairs; a year meted out by the calendar in a series of holidays, birthdays, and dinner parties, culminating in this final Labor Day weekend they agreed they couldn't possibly cancel. For the past five years, the same four couples had spent Labor Day at their Cape house. How could she and Mark spoil plans that had been made the previous fall? Also, there was a sense of keeping everything intact until they could tell the already suspicious children, who were spending their final vacation time with her parents in Connecticut. So they agreed to one last weekend together before she returned to their home in the suburbs and Mark to his newly rented apartment in Boston.

They made the usual preparations for weekend guests and promised no announcement until afterwards. They drove to the Cape in a haze of truce, stopping for oysters and to change drivers halfway there like old times. Once arrived, they swept out sand, washed towels, made beds, and hauled in bags of groceries. When Mark called, "Ilene, they're here, someone's coming along the road," there was excitement in his voice. She ran out to stand beside him, their shoulders bumping, the dune grasses waving around them. Oddly, this final secret collusion had produced a closeness they hadn't felt in years, and as the first couple drove up the steep hill into their charged atmosphere, the fragile wings of their secret fluttered in Ilene's chest.

By mid-afternoon on Saturday four couples had been installed in the guest rooms ("bunkrooms" was a more accurate description) and were taking a late-afternoon swim or starting an early cocktail hour. It took Ilene longer than usual to put away the offerings of food—always too lavish—like the fifteen-pound Virginia smoked ham from the Sandersons. The Sandersons were a formidably intelligent couple, trim, always referred to as "the Sandersons" and seemingly tethered to each other by an invisible ten-foot thread. Dotty and Hal Weisman carried in the largest moussaka that Ilene had ever seen. No doubt it would need refrigeration. Bernice and Alex West brought enough Branston Pickle, imported cheese, and exotic cold cuts to require an extra trip to the store for crackers and French bread. Ten pounds of pistachios and a single-malt scotch from Gail and Greg Reeder were being consumed with immoderate amounts of gin.

The women set the table and cooked while the men wiped off deck chairs and assembled windsurfing boards. After a dinner of moussaka and cold shrimp salad, people wandered out to the deck, abandoning coffee for a nightcap. A light breeze lifted the women's hair, made sails of their long cotton dresses drifting against their husbands' knees. Below, the scrub grass and brush whispered fitfully across the dunes.

The tide was either coming in or going out.

Mark unfolded more chairs and refilled glasses. They talked languidly of the past year, catching up on one another's kids and jobs and the subtle failures of successful lives. The Sandersons' clinic had taken on two new partners; Gail was up for tenure this fall; Alex was considering going to AA—next week; Hal reaffirmed his waning faith in Freud, not that anyone had challenged it; Mark minimized a lateral promotion with a shrug; Bernice had lost and gained fifteen pounds; Greg's company was going public.

Slouched in a low canvas chair, sandals off, Ilene listened to the murmur of satisfied voices. She almost forgot that she and Mark were acting—it was so easy. Perhaps she had been pretending for longer than she thought. Through her half-empty glass she gazed at the flat, calm bay below. Its blue net floated wide, as if to break the fall of the red, glowing sun.

When it came time to give the welcoming toast, Mark took Ilene's hands and pulled her gracefully to her feet, then stiffly flung his arm around her shoulders. Ilene pictured what their friends saw: an attentive husband embracing his suntanned wife, his arm pressing against the curve of her blond hair, their tanned faces smiling. Finally, glass raised, he ended with "Old friends together—friends forever." It brought sudden tears to Ilene's eyes because she knew he was promising her a friendly divorce, but the guests heard only that the weekend was officially under way.

Mid-morning of the next day, she found the broken porcelain soap dish resting on towels on the vanity shelf. As she was gluing the three large pieces together, searching for the correct tension to keep the edges fixed, Gail slid onto a stool and said ruefully, "Sorry. I break one of those a year, but they're usually my own."

"Forget it. Fix us a Bloody Mary," Ilene said, shrugging her shoulder toward the vodka. The weather had held, and the other guests were at the beach. Gail was Ilene's closest friend. Over the years, Ilene had confided in her and now alone together—Ilene fixing her broken dish and Gail slicing lemons for Bloody Marys—their old pattern of intimacy tempted Ilene to tell Gail her secret. She'd be the first person Ilene would call when she got home anyway. But something, perhaps the need for holding the pieces of the dish together so precisely, kept Ilene from saying anything. Besides, she and Mark were audience enough for each other's performances—although she suspected each couple would do a replay of the weekend with scintillating hindsight, separating the red herrings from the obvious clues.

Hal Weisman, her husband's tennis partner and a prominent shrink, was to be avoided. Once, the year before, he'd helped her carry dishes into the kitchen and asked "Ilene, how are you?" in such a concerned way that out of nowhere, while handing him plates of lemon tart, she'd started to cry. "I'mmmm—fiiiiiine," she'd said, weeping into a paper towel, and had told him so each time she sent him off with more servings of dessert.

It was Hal, the next day, who broke the outdoor shower. She heard him swearing and banging on the pipes below the deck where she sat reading. She put the *Times* aside and squinted down through the deck to see the chrome handle in his hand. Then he peered into his bathing trunks as if to determine how much sand he'd be tracking into the house. A lot. They'd have sand everywhere, which would make tiptoeing around in the night when she couldn't sleep more difficult.

Sadly, no plumber jokes came to Ilene's mind when Mark later tried to replace the shower handle. He had a wrench tucked into the waistband of his faded swimsuit and his bare back glistened with sweat. Ilene, still in a cotton shift, was holding the shower pipe steady. They'd been through countless projects like this one, a good team: Ilene standing by, handing Mark tools, steadying ladders; or Mark moving furniture, without complaint, as Ilene said here to there and sometimes "no, back like it was."

"How we doing?" Mark stage-whispered to her, grinning. "I feel like we're doing summer stock in Wellfleet Harbor Actors Theater. Prompt me if I forget my lines."

"Can you believe," she whispered back, "that no one's guessed?" Finally, when the handle seemed safely attached, Mark tried it out, drenching them both.

"It works," Ilene cried out, dancing backwards, lifting her skirt.

Mark followed and kissed her wet cheek. "Just has to last the weekend," he said, then rolled his eyes at his lapse of tact. But they both laughed, bringing Hal out to admire Mark's handiwork.

Later that night, as if for good old times, she and Mark made love. She realized she probably would never see him naked again—his rounded stomach with its appendix scar. Nakedness has a special vulnerability, and since their decision to divorce they'd sheepishly taken to donning an armor of clothes at bedtime—his pajama bottoms and her peach silk nightgown from when Stevie was born.

When she turned off her reading light, Mark heaved in an exaggerated turn to nestle against her back, his breath warm on her neck. The unaccustomed clothes and new shyness—his hand pulling up the soft drape of her gown, and her fingers tugging at the limp ties of his pajamas—made their final union gentle, sharp, high, and brief. There wasn't anything to say. At the end each laughed, as if embarrassed by the forgotten poignancy of a tenor sax in an unexpected song.

She was just falling asleep when something crashed in the bedroom below theirs. A sound of tearing timber. Ilene sat up, fumbling for the light. Mark kicked off the sheet. "Lord save me from insurance claims," he groaned.

They groped their way downstairs and followed the squeals and muffled giggles to the Sandersons' room to see them sprawled on the floor, clutching sheets and pillows against the backdrop of a splintered bed. An empty wine bottle sat on the window ledge. Laughing, the Sandersons explained that, well, it all just happened.

"Some orgy going on over there?" Gail yelled from across the hall.

"Need any help?" Hal called from the next room.

Mark said everything was under control. "I think."

The men lifted the headboard and frame, broken beyond repair, and carried the pieces out to the patio below the deck while Ilene looked for double sheets to make up the couch. The Sandersons gathered pillows and slippers, still laughing sheepishly. Ilene stretched the sheets over the mattress and said goodnight again, but instead of returning to bed she went out onto the deck, careful to avoid splinters, and leaned over the railing. The sky was a black bowl of stars, and below, the bay glistened in the moonlight, framed by dark rounded dunes and the shimmering necklace of Provincetown. Her legs were wet and cool. As she breathed the salt air, her gown drifted around her and she could smell that she had just made love.

The next day, on Labor Day, in rapid succession: Greg shredded the sunfish sail while showing off for the "girls" on the beach; Bernice accidentally upset the Scrabble game when Ilene won with 'eking' and four letters were lost in the sand; the CD player quit and voices seemed harsh without its soothing pulse; the laptop had been moved somewhere, though the cord was still plugged in beside the couch; two wine glasses lost their stems because someone loaded the dishwasher wrong. As Ilene searched around the spray attachment for broken glass she was grateful that the weekend was almost over.

That evening after the cookout of vodka, steaks, red wine, and gin, Dotty coaxed Mark to go on a moonlit walk under dire threat of a cold bath from the seltzer siphon bottle. "I'll come. I'll come," he said. He clutched a glass to his chest and cowered as Dotty aimed arcs of water at his back. Only Ilene watched them weave away. Hal and Greg were dealing with the deficit; the Sandersons were complaining about the rise in malpractice insurance and tuition costs to Gail, who nodded at intervals, her eyes closed. Bernice had gone to bed with a headache from two hangovers.

Sometime later, Mark and Dotty reappeared. Mark headed for the deck bar, his sweater woven with dry dune grass. Dotty reported in a slurred voice that somewhere on their walk, in a friendly tug of war, she'd surrendered too abruptly and couldn't remember where the siphon bottle had been abandoned, although she assured Ilene that it wasn't working right anyway. Swaying toward his wife, Hal tilted his glass, dumping ice cubes on the top of her head, explaining that Dotty needed a little cooling down. Dreamily, she shook her dark curls free of ice and bits of grass. Heavens, Ilene thought, what did men see in her?

Ilene waved the whole thing away but she didn't meet anyone's eyes. "Go to bed," Gail said to Dotty. "You need your beauty sleep." Hal took the cue and propelled Dotty toward their bunkroom. Mark shrugged through another drink, telling Alex about his brother's success with AA. Angry voices floated up from the beach where the Sandersons were searching for missing sandals.

Finally everyone went to bed with yawns too wide, and too much show of nonchalance. Ilene turned off the lights, then changed into her nightgown in the bathroom. The Sandersons were still sleeping on the living room couch, so Ilene was forced to retreat to the bedroom. Her reading lamp spotlighted her empty half of the bed. Mark was already hunched into his pillow, his face bloated and petulant. Her anger erupted as she shut the door.

"You could have waited," she said.

Mark opened one eye. "Go to bed."

"Everything will just go away, right."

"Shit. I'll never see Dotty again after this weekend," he said into the pillow. "Hal's a nerd."

"Hal's your goddamn tennis partner. Your best friend." Still standing, Ilene clicked off her light, then leaned against the window frame. She could smell Mark's unfinished scotch on the sill.

"Hal's still a nerd," he said.

The Cape night was black with clouds, the breeze damp. They should have called off the weekend. Surely their friends would have understood a cancellation more than this charade.

They all slept late and rose with headaches of varied intensity. The sun never appeared. The temperature put swimming out of the question— thank god. At first, they avoided each other—rummaging through rooms for shoes, sunglasses, scarves—trying to remember exactly what they'd said and done the previous evening, tentative with their "good mornings," until it was fairly well established that no one was going to make a scene. Alex offered to make coffee—and there went the Melior pot.

Finally, the guests departed two-by-two, half-heartedly calling out "Same time next year." The Sandersons, one pair of sandals declared lost, rattled away in their ancient Peugot, Penne. Ilene was glad she and Mark hadn't acquired the habit of naming things like cars, refrigerators or boats—Vishnu the Volvo, Wanda the washing machine—it would have been like parting with a slew of household pets. Gail gave Ilene a quick hug and even before their car had vanished down the road, Mark turned away. The wind had picked up from the east, pushing in a low grey sky.

As in the past, she and Mark separated into their pattern of divided duties. She cleaned the refrigerator and emptied the leftovers into coolers or garbage bags for the dump. Mark collected chair cushions and umbrellas and stacked them inside on top of folding chairs and deck tables. She sprinkled mothballs among the linens, found the computer under one of the bunk beds, reunited it with the charger. The washer whirred into action above the noise of winter shutters locking into place. Mark called their winter handyman and said that later in the week he should turn off the electricity, shut the water off and drain the pipes.

When most of this was done, Ilene poured a glass of white wine and sat on the high stool at the kitchen counter to make a list. She wrote:

To fix or replace:
Soap dish
Sunfish sail
Outside shower handle
Scrabble
Double bed
CD player
Seltzer bottle
Coffee pot.

There was something more, she felt sure. Clouds rolled past their hill as she tried to think. Maybe Mark would know. She called to him, then spotted him dragging the sunfish up from the beach. He wouldn't hear her. When she read the list again she saw that nothing really was that important. Most of it would never be replaced.

They packed separate suitcases separately. Ilene spread her suitcase out on their bare mattress, and Mark carried his into a bunkroom. He went back and forth cleaning out his closet and drawers while she retrieved hot clean clothes from the dryer, their paths crisscrossing as perhaps they always would. She folded blouses, skirts, shorts, tucked in underwear, belts, sandals. Her suitcase filled rapidly. She pictured Mark rolling his shirts into balls, slapping his pants into folds, zipping shut his shaving kit. He always had extra space in his suitcase—space she would have used if it hadn't been their last weekend.

Grief

Harris was walking his usual route to work, up Beacon Street and past the State House, when half a block ahead he saw their stolen car stopped at a red light. It was their missing car, all right—a white '94 Honda Accord, license plate 432 DOG, easy to remember—and it was still pumping out pale blue exhaust, portent, Harris recalled thinking, of a large muffler bill and so much grief.

He quickened his pace to get a look at the driver leaning against his door, the driver's fingers drumming impatiently on the wheel as if he had better things to do with his time and Harris's car than wait for the light to turn green. Or maybe the police cruiser idling two cars behind was making him nervous.

Harris ran back to the cruiser and rapped sharply on the window, passenger's side. It scrolled down at a snail's pace. Pointing, Harris told the cop, "See that car two cars ahead? The white Honda. That's my car. It was stolen two weeks ago. See it? That's my car."

As the light turned green, the Honda pulled away with the rest of the morning traffic. Bursts of adrenaline shot through Harris—the first thing he'd felt in the year since his wife's death.

The cop looked after Harris's disappearing Honda and then back at Harris as if trying to decide if he was a nut. "OK, Mister, get in," the cop said. For once Harris was grateful for the respectable-looking briefcase his wife had given him on their twenty-fifth anniversary.

Harris yanked on the door handle, but it was locked.

"No, in back," the cop said. "Get in the back."

Harris threw his briefcase onto the backseat and slid in behind what was surely a bullet-proof window, taxi-style. Siren blaring, they crept down Beacon Street in a low-speed chase and swung right on Tremont. Cars parted for them reluctantly—giving up feet, not yards.

Thirty seconds later they were bumper to bumper with Harris's stolen car and the cop was strongly suggesting on his loud speaker that the driver pull over. Harris was sitting forward, his nose inches from the scratched plastic divider. "That's it, that's my car," he said.

"You wait here," the cop said, as if Harris had been planning to accompany him on the dangerous stroll to the stolen car. Unbidden images came to Harris's mind. He pictured a stash of cocaine or a weighty little handgun the new owner had tucked under the driver's seat or hidden among their maps of New England and their hiking guides.

Now the cop was standing outside Harris's car, legs spread in cop-stance, no doubt asking to see the driver's license and registration. Good luck. The registration was in the glove compartment where it belonged, but hidden—his wife's idea—inside a paperback mystery involving root vegetables. The cop car's siren and flashing lights had drawn a business-suited crowd, which gathered at a safe distance from any potential mayhem.

Knowing Boston, Harris had never hoped to get their car back—and still road-worthy. He'd merely expected to come home to a message from the police on his answering machine saying they'd found his car trashed and wired on the campus of Tufts or MIT or abandoned in a bad part of town. The day after his wife died, he'd driven an hour west on I-90 until he came to a rest stop with a phone booth. He'd pulled the folding door shut against the outside world, and he'd called home over and over to hear her voice say, "Hello, please leave a message. We don't want to miss anything." Then he'd saved the tape and recorded a message of his own.

"No license on him," the cop said as he dropped into the front seat. "Says he left the registration with his sister cause she's trying to sell the car for him." He punched 432 DOG into a black box on the dash. Seconds later, like a fax—maybe it was a fax—out scrolled a sheet of paper with not much written on it, but the cop studied it thoroughly.

He verified Harris's name, address, and when he'd reported the car missing. Then once again he told Harris "wait here" and approached Harris's stolen car, where he motioned for the driver to get out. The crowd drew back.

The driver's Red Sox jacket had a ripped sleeve and his jeans were faded to a pale blue. Short and stocky, he was this side of forty, a limp ponytail hanging off a bald rump of a dome.

The cop spun him around and told him to lean against the car, his legs spread apart, then he patted Ponytail down movie-style before clamping handcuffs on his wrists. Satisfied, the cop pointed to where Harris sat waiting and gave Ponytail a slight nudge toward him. Soon Ponytail was peering in at Harris. His gaze was cool, not giving anything away. Static hissed on the cop's radio as the dispatcher asked if the cop wanted back-up. "Nah," the cop said through the front window, "I'm bringing him in."

Somehow Harris couldn't picture himself and Ponytail locked in, side by side, in the back seat. He tried to roll down the window but it wouldn't budge.

The cop nodded for Harris to get out—what else could his nod mean? Harris gathered up his briefcase and waited for the cop to open the door. Harris's peripheral vision assured him that Ponytail and he were not going to do anything rash like make eye contact a second time.

"The car's all yours," the cop said. "Keys are in it."

All three of them looked at Harris's car, helping the police cruiser hold up traffic. Their bottleneck was doing a bad job of channeling three lanes of angry drivers into two.

"Thanks," Harris said. Then, "You mean I just drive it away?"

"Anywhere you want," the cop said. "I can't take custody of him and your car at the same time. He's coming with me. I guess that leaves you with the car." His mustache twitched with humor, impatience, and pride.

"Sure thing," Harris said, something he knew he'd never uttered before in his life. "Well, see you around." Feeling a bit ridiculous, Harris took possession of his car. He moved the seat back and adjusted the rearview in time to see Ponytail disappear into the cop car, the cop's hand on the back of Ponytail's neck to make sure his head cleared the doorframe. The cop pulled out and around Harris, no siren but his lights still flashing.

Slowly, Harris drove back to his apartment and parked in front, in the same spot from which his car had been stolen. For the first time, he assessed its state—then set to gathering up Dunkin' Donuts cups, McDonald's cartons, and candy wrappers, and stuffed them into a white Dunkin' Donuts sack. The paperback mystery—*Roots of All Evil*—was still in the glove compartment, and just as his wife had predicted, had disguised the registration well. The hiking guides and maps were still under the seat; there was no handgun. And when Harris got home after work that night there was no wife to tell the story to.

Three days later, he was matching socks and watching the six o'clock news when the phone rang. He hoped it wasn't the solicitous new tenant from the upstairs apartment, a woman whose roast lamb and braised chicken tempted Harris to emerge from his solitary gloom—a gloom he always returned to well-fed but even more despondent. She had probably noticed his car in the street and wanted to hear how he'd got it back, perhaps to help him celebrate. He didn't know how to tell her that more than the car was still missing. When he said "Hello," he felt instant relief that it was not the woman upstairs, but a man's gravelly voice. "You got my TVs," the voice said.

Harris told him he had the wrong number.

"No I don't," he said. "I want my TVs."

Harris hung up and went back to sorting socks. Mostly black, they were draped over the back of the couch, side by side, toes pointing down, the way his wife used to line them up. Now, fewer and fewer of them matched. The phone rang again. It was probably the guy missing his TVs, and Harris thought, "Let him."

The next night, about the same time, the phone rang. Harris was sitting on the couch beside the leftover socks, again dreading the cheerful voice of the woman upstairs. A man's gravelly voice said, "They're in the trunk of your car."

"The TVs?" Harris said.

"See, I knew you had them."

Harris matched the man's TVs with his own stolen car. Ponytail. Knowing Boston, what had made Harris think Ponytail would be arrested, indicted, convicted, and put away? The cop never suggested to Harris that he should press charges, a failure pointed out by his cynical colleague in the accounting firm where Harris spent his days. "The cop probably dropped your Ponytail-guy at the next corner," Rentz had said. Clearly, Ponytail wasn't calling Harris now from some jail. Lord, Harris didn't need this. "Look—"

The man cut him off. "You got your car back safe and sound. No harm done. I just want my TVs."

"How did you get my number," Harris asked.

"Information," the man said. "AT&T."

"Someone's here," Harris said. "Can we talk about this another time?"

"You'll talk TVs tomorrow?"

"Tomorrow," Harris said and hung up, picturing Ponytail carless, standing in some phone booth near a bus stop or subway, figuring his chances. Harris put a Stouffer's lasagna in the oven and headed out to visit his car.

The car was where he'd parked it when he got it back four days ago. In the beam of his flashlight, he unlocked the trunk and found two TVs wedged in tight, just like the man had said. Harris had to admire the way he packed. With a sharp pang of regret he recalled his annoyance that his wife insisted on packing up the car for their camping trips. She'd assemble everything outside by the car, eye it thoughtfully, then begin with the large items first—the tent, the kerosene stove. At the end, there'd be no extra space, but nothing left behind.

The TVs weren't new, but newer than Harris's, with large blank screens. All of a sudden he felt very tired.

The next night he waited for the call, not sure what he'd say. He turned the news on with no sound. The back of the couch was free of socks, the socks put away. Who said they had to match? When the phone rang Harris was ready with a gruff hello, but this time it was the woman upstairs calling to say she'd just slipped a stuffed free-range roasting chicken into the oven and it was far too much for one person. It would be ready in about two hours. Cornbread and onion stuffing she said, and quite a bit of tarragon. Harris's wife had always used sage and rosemary. For what must have been the fifth or sixth time, Harris thanked her and said he'd bring a bottle of wine. He imagined the new photographs his upstairs neighbor would show him, her son's gourmet peppers, or alarming images from her daughter's latest assignment with Doctors Without Borders—a daughter who had his neighbor's same pale hair and deep-set, discerning eyes. He could hear his neighbor's stories of Sip, her cat, who coated his trousers with hair, her hints about a new movie she'd like to see at the theater down the block. He wouldn't tell her, and she couldn't know, that his wife and he had held hands in every movie they ever saw—her hand in his, their fingers changing pressure in her lap of wool, or denim, or silk. Often now, his hands felt empty. His neighbor couldn't know he was afraid, no, terrified, that in a moment of high emotion or fright at the images on the screen, he might reach for her hand—her perfectly good but achingly unfamiliar hand.

"I'll bring a bottle of white wine," he said, again because he didn't know how to say no. Then he clicked off the silent news and hauled out his briefcase. Two hours was enough time to get through tonight's office work.

Ponytail called five minutes later.

To Harris's surprise, he found himself taking part in complicated, delicate arrangements to give back the TVs. Of course, this was after Ponytail explained that they had once been in dire need of repair, but now they were ready to be returned to their impatient owners. "I pick up and deliver," he said. "This won't take long. You got any TVs, toaster-ovens, anything giving you trouble?"

"Just the TVs," Harris told him. They said goodbye.

Ten minutes later Harris was driving to the appointed place, wondering if he really would go through with this maneuver. Lately, he didn't feel prepared for anything. He probably wouldn't be meeting

Ponytail if his wife were at home waiting for him, worrying. They would have talked it over, together come up with a plan. It saddened him that he didn't know what she would have wanted him to do.

As arranged, Ponytail was standing on the corner of Government Center, near the subway stop, only a few blocks from the spot where Harris had recovered his car. Neither of them had suggested Ponytail come to Harris's house. Though the September night was warm, Ponytail's hands were tucked into the front pocket of his Red Sox jacket. This made Harris a little nervous. He pulled to the curb and beeped his horn twice. Ponytail glanced at Harris's car, and then, as if to shield himself from a brisk wind, he slowly turned full circle to light a cigarette behind cupped hands. Clearly, he was looking for a trap, and somehow his caution made Harris feel a little better. Finally, Ponytail sauntered over and leaned down as if to make sure it was Harris, then casually flicked away his cigarette and tugged on the handle of the passenger door. It was locked; Harris had made sure it was locked before setting off. Ponytail didn't seem to find the locked door strange and stepped back with a nod. Harris, embarrassed by his own unaccustomed display of caution, got out. His car idled in a light cloud of blue exhaust.

Across the roof, Ponytail squinted at him, straight in the eye. "Like I said on the phone, this won't take long. An hour maybe." He took his hands out of his pockets and placed them flat on the car's roof—as if to offer Harris, with this gesture, his assurance that he was not going to do anything rash. No doubt he was counting on the same from Harris.

"Okay," Harris said, thumping the car's roof with the flat of his palm. "Let's do it." Once again, adrenaline pumped through him as it had when he first spotted his car. He slid behind the wheel, unlocked the passenger door. Ponytail got in, the first passenger to ride in his car since his wife died. Although he'd never thought of his wife as a passenger. Ponytail's knuckles were white and his fingers drummed on worn denim knees.

"Where to?" Harris said, belatedly thinking he should have told someone—maybe the woman upstairs—where he was going.

"Get onto Storrow and head up Route 1." Ponytail buckled his seatbelt and slouched against the door, eyeing his side mirror, his ponytail a wisp on his solid shoulder. Stealthily, Harris rubbed the back of his neck, unable to imagine securing his hair with a rubber band, unable to feel a ponytail swishing against his collar, surprised even to consider it.

Once they were on the open road, Ponytail said, "Hear that rattle? Oil needs changing."

Harris glanced down at the dash which was reassuringly dark. "A light usually comes on if—"

"Them lights don't know nothing."

"So, you think it's the oil?" Harris said.

"I was gonna do it."

"Yes, well, thanks," Harris said.

"You probably know about the muffler," Ponytail said.

Harris told him he did. Then, "You been repairing TVs long?"

Ponytail thought for a moment. "Nah. Not too long. What do you do?"

"Mostly tax returns," Harris said.

"Repairing tax returns long?" Ponytail said.

Indeed, Harris thought, but only said, "Not too long." They settled into silence as the neon of roadside businesses flashed by. After a while, Ponytail told Harris to turn off Route 1 and take the overpass, then make a right at Cappy's Liquor. Three streets over they were in a neighborhood of two-story houses, lanky trees, and sloping, cracked sidewalks. Aluminum siding glowed in the evening's dusk. One house had a horizontal freezer on the front porch, another an old-fashioned gas oven. Harris had seen such things on porches before, but now they seemed strange and menacing.

"OK, first stop coming up," he said, trying for a little light-hearted humor. But it turned out—and why was he again surprised—that the TVs were going to one house. Ponytail's house.

"I said it wouldn't take long," Ponytail said, as if he was doing Harris a favor by consolidating the deliveries. They pulled into a narrow driveway bordered on one side by a chain-link fence. Lights were on in the downstairs of the house. A green pickup on cement blocks loomed off to the side. Now it was Harris's turn to think about a trap as Ponytail got out and slammed the car door. A jungle gym took up most of the small back yard.

Harris guardedly emerged from his car. Clothes flapped on a clothesline in the skinny side yard next to the driveway: blouses or shirts, workpants, kids' clothes, socks, and a long red dress or robe of some shiny material that caught the light from the street lamp.

Ponytail followed Harris's gaze. "Damn dryer's broken," he said. "Wife's been nagging me to fix it. I keep forgetting to order the part." At the fence, beneath a window, he gave a sharp whistle.

Harris backed up fast till he was flat against the car door with thoughts of taking off, TVs and all. Why on earth was he here?

As if on cue, a woman came to the window and peered out through the screen. She was jiggling a kid about two on her hip. Absurdly, Harris found himself noticing that her blonde ponytail was fatter than her husband's.

"Hey," Ponytail called out to her, his thumb jabbing the air in Harris's direction. "He's gonna help me put the stuff in the garage." Another kid, not much older, butted his head under her arm.

"Bring in the clothes when you finish," she said without acknowledging Harris, then smartly wheeled the children away.

"Let's get to it," Ponytail said.

His voice startled Harris, who had been imagining what it would be like to park in this driveway, to live in this house. With studied efficiency, Ponytail heaved up the garage door and turned on the light. "They're going in there," he said. With a jerk of his head, he indicated four saw horses covered with boards at the rear of the garage under a large, neat wall-board display of tools—most of which Harris didn't recognize—and three small blue cabinets of tiny drawers labled *screws* and *nails* and *nuts* and *bolts*. To one side, Harris could make out the sturdy shapes of five microwaves still in their shipping boxes and four spiffy new leaf blowers. Ponytail swiped the table with a rag—it was a kind of "no comment" gesture, and Harris was grateful for it.

Together, they hoisted the first TV out of the trunk. Hobbling sideways, they carried it up the driveway, arms wrapped under and around it, foreheads almost touching across its top.

"Set her down—right—here," Ponytail panted, wiping his face on his jacket sleeve. The TV was heavy. Harris's arms burned. He was out of shape from no exercise, no long hikes for over a year. They trooped back to the car for the last delivery.

"Done." Ponytail patted the second TV. Carefully, he spread a brown tarp over the TVs and microwaves, then turned off the light. Harris stood off to the side while he pulled down the garage door.

"Well—" Harris said, and because he didn't know what else to say, he turned toward his car. It had probably been parked on and off in this same driveway for three whole weeks. Beyond the fence, the red robe or dress was fluttering back and forth. Harris could see now that the hem was a little ragged and one of the elbows had a hole in it, but it was still of use. Without thinking, he walked past his car to the clothesline and reached up to undo the clothespins holding the robe in place. The robe was light and slippery as he folded it over his arm.

Ponytail touched his shoulder. "Hey man, you don't need to do that."

On the way home, Harris forced himself to drive slowly even though the upstairs neighbor was waiting for him. She'd want to know all about his getting the car back, so over dinner he'd recount how he'd spotted his car in traffic, and his surprise that it was still road-worthy. He'd tell her about the telephone calls, the tense drive up Route 1, the wife and kids at the window, the garage full of companionable leaf blowers, microwaves, and TVs. He'd tell her how, as he was pulling out of the drive, Ponytail had slapped the side of his car, hard, and Harris had jumped like he'd been shot, but Ponytail only wanted to tell him to "remember to check the oil." Then maybe somewhere along toward dessert, Harris would tell her more about his wife.

Deck

ON A SKIMPY MARCH morning, Cass reluctantly left Boston to check on the Cape house. She dreaded seeing the new deck they'd contracted for last fall, a reminder that life had gone on in the wake of her husband's death in December. Pulling into their driveway too fast, she almost hit the ugly dumpster that squatted there, normally a tight roost for two cars. It was eight, maybe nine feet long, and at least seven feet tall, with rusted vertical ribs. The carpenter wasn't around, nor was a final bill tucked inside the unlocked door.

After lugging her duffel and two grocery bags into the kitchen, still in her boots, she clumped down the long hallway to the sliding glass doors that opened out on to the deck to check on Eddie's work.

There was no deck.

There was only a twelve foot drop to the ground where sand and wisps of sea grass churned in the wind off the bay. Grey dimpled snow still edged the foundation, and the scrub pines looked defeated under the overcast sky. The dismantled deck must be in that dumpster. She bowed her head against the cold glass of the sliding doors and cried.

That deck had been the center of life here in their Cape house. She pictured Bloody Marys on the table between their deck chairs, Sunday papers blowing around their knees. Trevor's tripod leaning against the rail and seventeen-year old Ben changing the strings on his guitar, telling them about the Bryan Sutton concert he'd gone to that weekend. Surely parts of the deck were still in the dumpster. If only Eddie could return it to its original battered self.

Numb with cold, she dragged the aluminum ladder from the garage and hoisted it against the dumpster's edge. She hoped the neighbors wouldn't come out to welcome her back. They were drinks-once-a-summer neighbors who had called her in Boston to offer condolences, but for sure she didn't want to revisit their sympathy from a ladder.

She climbed up one rung, two rungs, till she rose above the metal lip and could peer inside.

A white toilet glowed against the gray boards of the old deck. Irrationally, she made a mental inventory of their bathrooms. Of course the toilet wasn't theirs. Eddie was redoing someone's bathroom elsewhere. She pictured him hauling the toilet here, straining to lift it out of his truck bed and heaving it in a white arc over the top.

When Eddie didn't answer his cell, she left no message. He'd see that she had called. She built a fire in the woodstove, put groceries away, and yanked sheets off the furniture. After changing into a nightgown, she dragged a chair in front of the stove and watched the logs sputter and shift.

So, here she was. Without Trevor. She'd been alone when she bought this house because Trevor, after several trips, had given up, but told her she should keep looking. It was a treehouse, sort of, with three floors of oddly-shaped rooms and decks. The real estate agent said a loony professor had hired MIT grad students, protégés of architect Maurice Smith, to build it according to his concept of an inside-out house—the outdoor spaces an extension of the inside design. That day, she'd made an offer on the house sight unseen by Trevor. Then she'd quickly sketched the three floors, something her students at the architectural school couldn't do worth a damn though they could create impressive digital renderings. "Our Cape house," she said, rolling out her drawings on Trevor's Boston desk. He'd marveled at her find. "All those windows. Seven different roof lines?" He was such a believer.

On a sweltering afternoon in August, Eddie had knocked on their door and asked if they had any projects he could do. He'd built their outdoor shower earlier that summer, so they knew his work. When Trevor asked what he had in mind, Eddie said well, maybe build your wife here a studio. Or a larger main deck. Cass didn't want a studio, but a larger deck was something they had considered. After hearing Eddie's sorry assessment of the Cape economy, his needy crew, his kids without shoes—here he had the grace to grin—they had agreed on a new deck. Ten minutes later, they stood on the old deck sipping Coronas as Eddie drew a diagram in the air with the neck of his bottle. "Add at least ten more feet in these two directions. Get more furniture. A bigger grill." He pointed at their old Weber. "Change to gas." When his enthusiastic voice drew Ben out of his room, Eddie greeted him, saying, "And for sure you'll need safer railings when that son of yours has kids."

Ben snorted, and Trevor and Cass nodded their agreement, anticipating future birthdays, anniversaries, graduations, an inflatable plastic swimming pool for Ben's toddlers.

"I'll start the minute you move back to Boston. Take just under a month," Eddie said. He left happy—with a sizeable check in his pocket.

"He still has a mullet," Ben observed that evening, with the deadly fashion sense of a high school senior. His own hair was shaggy above freckles and Trevor's deep set, discerning eyes. "*Mullet* is a word I hope to forget," Trevor had said.

Three months later Ben elbowed Trevor's heart monitor aside to stand closer to his hospital bed, his fingers flicking the guitar pick he was never without. "The neighbors called to say someone's been over at the house," Ben said. "Eddie, maybe?" Cass admired Ben's attempt to keep his father tethered to the world a little longer.

A brief light glimmered in Trevor's eyes. "About time he got started," he said. Then he said he hoped the party after the memorial service would take place on the new deck. When Ben objected to the word party, Trevor assured him there always was one. "No gooey casseroles on that new deck. Only good food and better wine."

Ben, his voice breaking, said, "Can we have beer. Craft beer?"

That morning, the doctor had suggested that Cass arrange hospice care. No need to say the end was near.

Ben said goodbye and reluctantly left for school. Trevor weakly waved. Cass carried out the luncheon tray whose servings of food Trevor had merely spread around.

"What are you doing?" he said, his voice hoarse. Draw something, he'd told her, looking around, waving weakly at all the gadgets surrounding his bed, pointing to his feet, to the bouquet of tulips from the Lamson's. "Remember our discovery about the hibiscus flower on our visit to the Lamsons?" he said.

"Puerto Vallarta. Five years ago. Your new camera." When she lifted his cool hand, he turned his own palm down, his spread fingers covering hers.

"Do you remember my first time-lapse photo?" One day he had set up her tripod and trained the camera's eye, calibrated to take a photograph at forty-second intervals, on a hibiscus flower, a flower their host said only lives for one day. Sure enough, by noon the flower's face was fully open to the sun, its lush scarlet petals spread wide against its green leaves, alive and elegant and proud. Then, to their astonishment, as the afternoon waned, the flower used its last moments of life to slowly gather itself into the perfect cone in which it had begun the day.

"I feel like that flower," Trevor said, his fingers momentarily strong, his gaze a spark of heat before he closed his eyes. "Oh, Cass. I don't have anything left. It is taking all my energy to die."

Now, her coat hiding her nightgown, Cass backed her car out past the dumpster and fled back to Boston, her mind unspooling all the firsts without Trevor that lay ahead. It was taking all her energy to live.

"Lucky you weren't stopped by the cops, " Ben said, eyeing her nightgown.

Cass told him no deck yet, dropping her duffle inside the kitchen door.

"And The Mullet?" Ben asked.

"He never showed up," Cass said, and described the dumpster and the demolished remnants.

"What the hell." Ben's own sorrow flared and spent itself at random moments: wearing Trevor's old fishing vest after school; learning the intricacies of the intervelometer; playing his guitar in Trevor's study—plaintive minor chords.

The next day Cass called Eddie's cell and, when he answered, asked in a strained voice how work was progressing.

"Work's coming along fine," he said, breathing hard as if he'd been carting boards to the new deck in a snow squall that had gone unreported in Boston. "Too bad you can't take a run down here and see for yourselves."

Hers would have been a tantrum born of grief, so she did not tell Eddie that she'd been to the Cape the day before, that she had seen the toilet in the dumpster, and that clearly the progress he referred to was happening someplace else.

"You got carpenter ants," he said. "In the South wall."

"South wall?" Cass repeated. Unbidden came the memory of the sun setting as they drank their nightly martinis.

"And that big pine tree that grew so close to the old stairs," he said. "It's gotta go or we build the deck around it. It's healthy. I can do that easy."

Impatiently, she rose to pace her kitchen. How could she think about building around something—even a pine tree's ornately ugly branches—when each day she had to build around Trevor's absence, to decide how to live in the space he'd left behind in their two houses, in her mind and heart.

"Fine. Do it." She told him she'd be moving to the Cape the first week in May, and guests would be there later in the month. She didn't add that the guests were Trevor's parents coming for the memorial service.

"I'll be gone way before then," he said. "Way before then."

"Good," she said. The dumpster never came up.

In April the dumpster was still there. The toilet had been joined by a white porcelain sink.

"Tell Trevor ants got into the east wall, too," Eddie said. "So, I did that wall."

They were standing in the kitchen, looking out the sliding glass doors to where the deck should have been. Earlier that day, she'd placed two chairs in front of the doors as a reminder of the sheer drop immediately outside. It was time to tell him. So she described the surprise diagnosis of Trevor's illness, the trajectory of its rapid descent, and then his death.

Shocked and stricken, Eddie sank into one of the chairs as if she'd placed them there for this occasion; it felt impolite not to take the second chair. She could see him thinking that he and Trevor were roughly the same age. He began rubbing the back of his neck.

"We all just never know," he lamented, and went on to say that Trevor had been a good, good man. His eyes were shiny, his nose red. She couldn't imagine them crying together.

In desperation she said, "New haircut?"

Eddie's gaze took in her short tangled curls, and then once again his hand moved to his neck where the soft fringe used to be. "Oh yeah. I'm surprised I don't miss it. My wife—my ex-wife, that is—said I always petted it as if it were a kitten just before I stepped up to bat. Hyannis softball league," he said.

Alarmed, she imagined spring baseball practice, league games, strident coaches making imperative demands on his time.

Noting her alarm, he said, "Ken's back from Florida next week, and the lumber order is due in at the yard about then." He'd clearly forgotten telling her the lumber had come in last month. What would Trevor have said? He'd have been amused but said nothing. So she said nothing now.

Eddie was still thinking about Trevor. "Must be hard losing your husband early like that. So fast. Young, too." His self-conscious sympathy, it turned out, was prelude to how hard it was for him to see his ex-wife around town with her new guy. "They come to the games. Maybe gone is better."

As if required to do so, she tried to picture Trevor squiring around a new woman. It wasn't useful and Eddie saw that immediately. "Maybe not," he said. "Just different."

•

Cass left to attend a conference in Seattle. Ben was working on his eulogy with dogged dedication, sending Cass his thoughts in daily texts. Trevor's college roommate had offered to officiate at the service. Cass didn't know whether to dread or welcome all the anecdotes that people would tell about Trevor, how Trevor always did the unexpected. If he'd had to deal with her death and the missing deck he'd probably have dragged their friends out to the empty spot and reported that when Cass died she had taken the deck with her.

She stopped overnight in Boston to retrieve clothes, books, files. It was now May and Ben had been down to the Cape with friends. Cass was hoping for good news. "How does the new deck look?"

"Use your imagination," Ben said. Then "never mind, you'll see," and he refused to say more.

Cass drove through a nor'easter, the rain coming down in sheets, her shoulders tense with apprehension. Once more, she had to steer past the dumpster's rusty bulk. Automatically she hit the remote to open the garage door, and almost drove into a gleaming table saw surrounded by stacks of lumber. But not lumber for her deck; more like flooring for a fancy kitchen. Sawdust blew around in tiny whirls. The off/on switch was a cautionary red. Jesus Christ, Eddie had turned her garage into his workroom. She ought to charge him rent. He probably took afternoon naps in the house.

Once inside, she pulled the wicker chairs away from the sliding doors and opened them wide to the sheer drop below. Rain doused the pines as her second martini conjured up what surely would have been Trevor's incredulous delight at Eddie's nerve. She imagined Trevor saying, with real admiration, "We'll hold his table saw hostage so he has to come back." Oh how she missed his way of being in the world.

The next morning when she heard the whine of the table saw, she rushed outside, clutching her bathrobe tightly around her. "I told you I have a goddamn deadline," she yelled.

Eddie's face was tanned from working in the sun on someone else's roof or deck. He nodded silently, but he didn't raise his eyes from the board he was cutting—a board actually meant for her deck. Ken was sorting nails and also didn't meet her eyes.

"The deck has to be done in the next two weeks. And that dumpster—," she couldn't finish.

He finished for her. "—will be gone."

The entire week she couldn't look as he and Ken cut and hauled lumber around to the back of the house, and she refused to admire how they wove in and out of the pines. A friend dropped by with a borrowed book, and asked about the deck's progress. Cass's peripheral vision alerted her to Eddie's presence just outside the sliding glass doors.

"Don't even glance that way," Cass warned, taking her arm and turning her away from the scene. "I do not want to introduce you. I do not want to stand and chat. I do not want him to stop work for an instant."

Two days later, she returned from errands and a swim in Duck Pond to find the dumpster gone, replaced by a bare, moldy spot. Once curious about its delivery, she was dismayed that she'd missed its departure. The driveway looked enormous, almost cavernous. The garage was empty of table saw and tools.

The deck was done.

It stood nine feet above the carpet of pine needles, and its floor of grey boards stretched twenty by thirty feet across. Three sides of the house gave it shelter and shape, and the railings were safe even as their design rendered them almost invisible. She was walking the perimeter in amazement when Eddie appeared on the path below and climbed the stairs to join her, saying he'd dropped by to see what she thought. A six-pack from a local brewery dangled from his left hand.

The new deck had been built for late afternoon drinks with Trevor, but it would be cold beer with Eddie instead.

They hauled chairs from the garage as Eddie narrated the story of demolishing the deck, finding the carpenter ants, juggling the surprising amount of other work that had come his way—two kitchens in Truro, a roof in P'town. "But we got it done," he said raising his glass to hers in a toast. "I'll be at the memorial service. Trevor was a good man. Good to me. And he'll be missed."

When Eddie left, she kicked off her shoes and tucked her skirt above her knees to feel the evening breeze. Ben would be arriving soon, and a week later the guests for the memorial service. Trevor's absence would be the most felt presence of all, and it would never leave her. They had loved this house with its ragged view of the bay, and had marveled at how their landscape never changed with the advent of summer or the approach of fall. The scrub pines always loomed in the salty mist from the bay's cool waters, though soon their pollen would dust everything a pale and silken yellow.

The Mystery of Mistakes

GINA GAVE THE KEY to her daughter to unlock her lover's house. Gina's arms were full with his bicycle helmet and hiking gear. "Pull—pull the knob slightly toward you," she said. Gina remembered Galen's instructions from her first time here, six years before, and his loving note—in neat handwriting she now considered cramped—that said "mi casa es tu casa."

Finny swept the door open. "And we are in!" She gestured for Gina to enter first. "What if he's in bed with a cold?"

"He's a masochist. He'd be in the classroom with a cold," Gina told her. She had counted on the fact that mid-morning on Wednesdays he was always at the college.

"Okay. Now what?" Finny said, tucking the key into Gina's pocket.

Grateful for Finny's matter-of-fact attitude, Gina told her that first they would bring in Galen's stuff and dump it in the couch area, then gather up hers to take home.

"Got it," Finny said, and went back outside to begin unloading the car. Alone, Gina held Galen's red helmet against her cheek to breathe in the scent of his sweat, the cologne he always wore. Finally, as she set his helmet on the back of his reading chair, she realized that she had wanted to be in this house one more time.

"Mom?" Finny was back. She dumped a box on the couch.

"I'm good," Gina said, because she had to be.

Together, they made several trips to carry in clothes, dopp kit, frayed tennis shoes, manuscripts, books, Galen's second clarinet. Finny showed no interest in any of his things, but she unabashedly peered around, as if assessing her mother's past life here with her lover. Maybe comparing it to her own recent romance. Then she gave a shrug as if dismissing it all.

"I recognize some of your stuff," Finny said, rolling up a vest that Gina had left draped over a dining room chair. "I mean, shit, how much stuff is there?"

"I hate the word 'stuff'," Gina said, ignoring "shit." Why hadn't she made this trip alone? So far, Finny had been little comfort. But is that what she'd brought Finny for—comfort? Or to ward against any temptation Gina might have to wait for Galen's return?

"As in *low on stuff*," Finny snorted. "Point it out. I'll carry."

A week ago, Galen had suggested that they meet halfway between Boston and Providence to trade belongings. He'd been unfaithful in a serious way. She'd been unfaithful too, but less seriously. She felt moderately bad about this. He said it was time to break up. He'd offered to pack up all her belongings that had found their way to his place and asked her to do the same with his. They'd meet halfway between their homes. She told him her schedule for the next two weeks made this impossible, but she'd get back to him. She wasn't sure why his proposal felt unseemly, more so than this surreptitious trip on her own.

Last night, she'd called Finny to coerce her into joining her on the drive from Boston to Providence and back—three or four hours total. It took two phone calls. Her first request with no particulars got a quick "Nope, can't do it." Miraculously, after Gina's second call, Finny grudgingly agreed, saying Max would be busy the next few days. Recently, Finny had been giving her grief. Abrupt goodbyes on the phone. Cancelled dinners. Complaints about her brother and her father, Gina's ex-husband, whose actions she seemed to attribute to Gina. Not sure what this was about, Gina hoped it wasn't about Finny's latest man.

She picked her daughter up at eight on the dot, with two coffees-to-go. Finny took after Gina—curly golden hair, thin slivers of eyebrows, a full mouth.

"Did this goddamn mystery trip have to be so early," Finny said, yanking open the car door. "And why couldn't you go yourself like you've done a million times before." She stopped short when she took in the sight of the crammed back seat.

"Coffee?" Gina said.

Finny settled her backpack on top of Galen's duffle. "Never mind," she said and planted a hello kiss on Gina's cheek. Neither had bothered with lipstick.

Zooming along the highway she'd traversed countless times, she told Finny her story's ups and downs, finally and reluctantly including a brief summary of their infidelities.

At that Finny said, "So? So what?"

"What do you mean 'so what'?"

"Well, they're a symptom not a cause, right? I mean what makes a relationship fail? Dumb word, 'relationship'."

Sleepless nights hadn't quite provided Gina with definitive answers, either to the distant past with Finny's father, or now. The proverbial straw could be many things. Finny nodded when Gina mentioned Galen's "self-absorption" and "frugalities"—his insistence that all concert and theatre seats should be in the balcony, and his injunction against cutting a bouquet for their table from the profusion of tiger lilies in his yard. Oh. She remembered saying "oh" too often to his pronouncements. Then there were his bitter references to his mother's "voice in his ear." Gina pictured that voice floating above his shoulder, a voice as large and concrete as the lamp on his bedside table—always there. "Does Gina's hair have to be that curly?" he reported his mother as saying, and "She does have a large bosom." He alleged her judgments were a major grief to him, but Gina had come to recognize his mother's voice in his too many times.

Her eyes on the road, Gina could feel Finny studying her for wobbles and tears. She told Finny that in turn he'd probably found her too extravagant, maybe too uncomplicated?

Satisfied with Gina's sturdy assurances, Finny put her feet up on the dash and said, "I never liked Galen and his know-it-all-attitude anyway."

Gina silently took this in, leaving room for more, so Finny continued. "Even though he did seem to know it all, if you get what I mean."

Gina nodded that she did. She still might love him a little, but as the cliché goes, she probably didn't like him anymore.

Finny added, "I mean, intelligence can be intoxicating." A beat later, she laughed and said, "I almost said *even* intelligence…" At this they both laughed meanly. Finny tilted her head at the packed back seat. "So, I take it we're making a delivery," she said.

"It will all be dead on arrival," Gina said.

"Oh god, this has the makings of another family story I could do without," Finny said.

"So, do without. What about you and Max?" Gina had asked.

"Could we just make this trip about you," Finny said, putting her head back and shutting her eyes.

After dumping the rest of Galen's stuff in the living room, Gina gave Finny a quick, unembellished tour of the house. She marveled at how strange her continued sense of proprietorship was. Finny must have heard it in her voice, and followed her, petulantly opening drawers and slamming them shut, pushing at doors. First, the efficient kitchen with—well, there it was—two mugs beside the stove.

Finny gave one of them a push. "Did you ever consider that some woman might be here?"

"Foolishly, never," Gina told her, and quickly ushered her toward the downstairs study. Gina hoped she hadn't noticed the plastic honey bear beside the sink, its plump bear arms folded complacently over its plump bear belly. It was one of Gina's idiosyncrasies. She disliked bottles of dish soap with their promises of domestic happiness—Joy, Soft Comfort, Dawn. Her family had been washing dishes with "honey" for years. How long ago had she given the honey bear to Galen? Not "presented" it, but merely replaced his ugly bottle of dish soap with a bear she filled with honey-colored liquid. Now the liquid was a putrid blue.

"This was my study," she said, and pointed at her shelves of books. An empty shelf caught her unawares, as the half-filled box of books on the floor below testified to Galen's intent to exorcise the house of her.

"Looks like our boy got started," Finny said, giving the box a sharp kick.

"We're going to finish," Gina said. She pointed to her old PC on the desk, papers scattered here and there.

Then, hardening her heart, she led the way upstairs to his chaotic study with its books and music stands, his collection of antique recorders, CDs everywhere, clothes hanging from his desk chair, even an unpacked suitcase splayed open on the floor from a trip they took to London a month ago. "The CDs with 'G' on them are mine," she said.

"He's sure not a neatnik," Finny said.

"He said we have the same tolerance for mess," she told Finny. Though he meant the degree of untidiness in their houses, not their lives, where this observation had proved to be untrue. She would miss traveling with him, his adventurous itineraries, bear sightings in Newfoundland, their back road wanderings in British Columbia, belatedly reading the guidebook's injunction—no dirt roads without a winch. He had been mostly patient when she stopped to sketch a detail of a Gaudi tile in Barcelona or a sleeve of a girl's dress in a Dutch painting in Bruges. Some things she tried not to think about, like the bedroom across the hall where, in the first years they were together, he used to sing to her in bed.

Finny glanced at the rumpled blue spread, the flat pillows, as if dismissing them along with any thoughts they might have led her to entertain. "I only heard him play the clarinet once," Finny said, studying Gina closely.

"Once was enough." Gina filled Finny's arms with sweaters and skirts, and sent her down the stairs, staying behind to mourn the tiny concerts, his talent for going down on her, his blessings in bed. Lost.

She gathered up a pen from her bedside table, books, two pairs of reading glasses, dismayed that another woman was witness to their practicality. She swiped down her blue silk bathrobe from its hook—to be washed clean of him.

"Done up here," she called, her voice breaking as she descended the stairs, blue silk flapping against her legs.

Finny emerged from Gina's study with a box of books topped off with a green yoga mat. "I'm surprised at how much I recognize. You have two yoga mats."

"Could we please avoid an inventory," Gina said.

"But you really lived part of your life here," Finny said, her sharp elbow opening the front door. Letting it slam shut.

So part of her life was gone? Over? Gina gathered and packed. Finny carried.

Gina went from room to room, pointing at items to be taken out to her car: laptop, shelves of books, manuscripts, hair-dryer, CDs, yoga mat, racy lingerie she stuffed into a bag, Scrabble, coffee mugs, a tape dispenser, an Iron Clad roasting pan. They had agreed not to return any gifts, though Gina wished she had the nerve to take the ivory-handled magnifying glass she gave him for Christmas.

She did feel petty as she tucked the roasting pan into a box, but he could buy his own. Same with the dehydrator she'd given him for drying mushrooms. He was an amateur mycologist and she would miss the magic of a questionable mushroom's spore prints appearing on a white paper towel. She'd have to use that in a story someday. Then she remembered what she had not brought back of his—the unpublished novel. Where was it? He had resurrected it when they first met, revised the ending, and ceremoniously handed over the manuscript for her to read. When she inquired, as she had learned to do, "Do you want comments and suggestions, or shall I read for entertainment," he said entertainment. She read all 600 pages, kept her misgivings to herself and assured him, not without a grain of truth, that she was entertained. When three dozen agents had turned it down, he said with no irony, "Perhaps your comments, now." But it was too late.

Finally, his house was scoured clean of her stuff.

Room by room, they did one last walk-through. Gina stood in each room's center as Finny orbited around her, pushed chairs sideways, swished curtains askew.

"Aren't these yours?" Finny held up a pair of Gina's hiking boots for rescue.

Gina nodded. Do women ever hike alone? Not without a dog. No dog. "I wouldn't not have done it, not had these years," Gina said. It sounded like the truth, but she had been known to lie to herself. She looked to see if Finny believed her. Finny nodded that she understood, probably from experiences with her last two men. She was in a relationship now going on its third monogamous year, but it was a troubled one that Gina suspected would die in the next few months. Gina's divorce from Finny's father when she was only seventeen certainly held no lessons. Finny took the hiking boots, still caked with mud from the Appalachian trail, out to the car and returned fast as if to keep Gina on track.

With Finny trailing after her, Gina looked for a place to leave the key, and settled on the middle of the desk that had been hers.

"No note?" Finny said, leaning against the doorframe. "Dear Know-it-All-Asshole." Expecting Gina's sure objection to that word, she rolled her eyes and was clearly surprised when Gina said, "Asshole gets no note."

Finny said she'd drive. Gina was dismayed that the car was so full—the remnants of her failed relationship obscuring the mirror's rear view.

As they were leaving Galen's driveway, Finny said "shit," and put her foot to the brake. "I knew you should have kept the key. But never mind, I can go in through a window. You left something behind."

Ignoring Gina's protests, Finny efficiently twisted up her long hair and pulled the elastic off her wrist to secure it. She meant business. She left the car running and slammed the door.

As Gina watched in dismay, Finny easily pushed in the old-fashioned screen next to the front door and with a vigorous gymnastic maneuver, dove in headfirst. Then she waved grimly, replaced the screen, and disappeared. In ten seconds flat, she reappeared empty-handed, but with a lump in her left jacket pocket that Gina couldn't make out.

"I saved it, so now it's mine," Finny said. Her "mine" was

underscored by how emphatically she squealed out of the drive.

"If it belongs to me, I get to decide," Gina said. "So, what is it?"

"No you don't. You left it there. Left it in that weasel's care. Abandoned it."

"Enough. There's bound to be mistakes in your future if the past two years are any clue."

"So now it's a mistake," Finny countered. "You said you'd do it again."

"That's the mystery of mistakes," Gina said. For the second time she regretted bringing Finny along. As if she needed to set an arrow arcing into the future without Galen, but with a loving, devoted daughter in her life. Sure.

"Whatever you're thinking about Max and me is probably true," Finny said a bit later as she drove into a Dunkin' Donuts. Then, "Remember this?" She wiggled the plastic bear that had once held honey in front of Gina's nose. "How could you give him this?" Finny accused her, as if only now she realized the breadth of Gina's life with Galen.

"You are damn well old enough to know why," Gina said, through a crumpled tissue. How could such a silly thing make her cry, but she was crying solid tears.

"You loved him," Finny said, tapping the blue bear on top of the steering wheel. She was crying now too, maybe fearing what lay ahead for her.

"You can have his goddamn bear. It's yours," she told Finny, but she held out her hand and Finny let her have it. "This awful blue is Dawn. Throw it out and buy your own Joy." She settled the blue bear in the cup holder, where it sat Buddha-like.

"Nice. My own fucking joy."

As Finny pulled out into traffic, Gina wondered what she made of this, her mother's fractured life. Would she be a stronger young woman, wiser than her mother, or fearful for her own future? Maybe more realistic about love. No, Gina shouldn't wish that on anyone. And what would Galen think when he returned to find they had been ransacking his house. What would he notice first? His stuff in the living room, of course. But then the empty bookshelf beside the couch, the tomb-like space in the front hall closet? He would find the key when he went into her study—no, now *the* study. Would he miss the blue bear?

What she did not imagine on this sad drive home was that later that evening he would call her. After first objecting to her raid on his house, he would weep and plead with her to give them another chance, say that they were too hasty in breaking up, pledge his undying love. Slowly, their stuff from that road trip's adventure migrated in reverse. Finny had the grace not to turn their trip into a story—yet—but she did not offer to return the bear. A month later, from the height of a new wisdom acquired during her own break-up, she told Gina, "No bear. You and Galen won't last." And Gina was afraid it was true.

Trips

"HERE'S ONE FOR YOU," Tucker says to Rick and Jen, Rick's fiancée. "How many hundred dollar cars would it take to drive to Cleveland?"

Rick squints at his older brother's new scraggly beard, which makes him look like a professor. As of last spring, Tucker *is* a professor. "Going from Boston to Cleveland?" Rick repeats.

"Right. You buy a car for a hundred dollars, drive till it dies, buy the next car," Tucker says.

Rick listens to see what Jen will say. She comes through with, "So the hundred dollars is a given?" She and Tucker are meeting for the first time. An hour ago, she arrived with lunch: a coarse duck pâté and two kinds of smelly, promising cheese.

"One hundred flat. That's the fun of it," Tucker assures her. Yesterday, he flew in from Chicago, a surprise visit on his way to a global warming conference in Brazil. Outside, a serious rain is keeping windshield wipers and umbrellas in motion, also keeping them drinking inside Rick's two–room apartment, stepping over thick textbooks and dog-eared law journals. Rick passes Tucker another beer, adding to the sizeable dent in the case of Sam Adams. "Jen?" Rick waggles a bottle but she shakes her head. She's been spreading pâté on crackers and passes one to Tucker.

"Do they even sell hundred dollar cars?" she asks, clearly suspecting otherwise. Her long auburn hair is down and coils around her neck, falling over her left shoulder. Rick likes to rest his hand on its cat-like warmth. She is talking about getting it cut, and already he misses it.

"Sure they do," Tucker says, scooping up a runny wedge of cheese.

"Course, there'll be no heat, no air, muffler probably gone, rusted floors, transparent fan belt, two hundred thousand miles minimum. Only worth a hundred." Then he reminds Rick how his roommate freshman year bought an old junk heap just before spring break for a hundred dollars. "The blue Chevy? The one you had to hit the starter with a hammer?"

"Hell, that Chevy would probably sell for three hundred today." Rick is glad to think of something other than his killer class on briefs and torts, wedding rings, and the burgeoning guest list.

"Where?" Jen asks. "Where do they sell hundred dollar cars?"

"Anywhere," Tucker says. "Car lots for starters."

"But what comes after 'starters'?" Jen says.

People usually don't question Tucker, so Rick is enjoying Jen's persistence. He and Jen met last fall in Merger Contracts and fell into bed, then into love during study sessions with three other people. They will graduate in May, and are planning an August wedding. Their engagement was announced over Christmas when Tucker was in Ecuador—land of lost gold, gathered in vain by the Incas as ransom for the freedom of Atahualpa, their king. When the conquistadors killed him anyway, the Incas reclaimed their gold and hid it—never to be found. Maybe Rick and Jen will go treasure-hunting in Ecuador some year. All last fall, the family made complicated, detailed plans to join Tucker there for the holidays, but with one thing and another—their sister's recital, their father's blood pressure—their conference calls about Ecuador came to nothing. Jen was annoyed that plans had fallen through so late they hadn't been able to get cheap tickets to her parents' home in Vancouver.

"Hundred-dollar cars are everywhere," Tucker said. "Any time you see a car parked on some front lawn, its nose sniffing at the road, sure bet it's For-Sale-by-Owner. It's that way in every country in the world. Slovenia, Australia, you name it. Usually in front yards with lawn ornaments—pink flamingos, ducks with their asses bobbing in the wind."

Jen rolls her eyes at Rick, who looks away. Moves not lost on Tucker.

"You'll see," Tucker tells her. "I'll buy the first car." Then to Rick, "Come on, man, wrap your lawyer's mind. How many hundred dollar cars will it take to drive from Boston to Cleveland?"

Jen is still in cross-examination mode. "OK. One car breaks down, you buy the next one?"

"For sure going to Cleveland will take more than one car," Tucker says. He is gleeful as he pokes the cheese plate at Rick. Rick heartily agrees that only one car would be a drag. "Dullsville," Tucker adds. To egg him on, Rick says he can imagine it taking eight, ten cars, and Tucker nods in quick little brush strokes.

But why Cleveland Jen wants to know? She has put her glasses on as if to read a map—or Tucker.

"Why not Cleveland?" Tucker says.

"That's not the same thing at all," Jen says. She looks from one brother to the other. "Do you two know anyone in Cleveland?"

"We definitely do not know anyone in Cleveland," Rick says. She'll be good in court, he thinks. Relentless.

"So why not Nashville or Detroit?" Jen says.

Tucker is adamant that it has to be Cleveland. He even laughs adamantly. Rick goes to the fridge for more beer as Jen takes another tack, asking Tucker if he's going to leave all those junk heaps by the side of the road? "Global warming but not recycling?"

Tucker's eyes widen to look at her appreciatively, then he nods his head at Rick. "No, no. You're right, the environment deserves better," Tucker tells her. "Hell, the cars deserve better! We'll get them towed to the next town. We'll have to get there anyway. One of us must belong to Triple A." Then he says he bets they don't know about the museum called the International Towing and Recovery Hall of Fame in Chattanooga. "Model T wreckers-in-action." Rick believes it. He's always admired Tucker's capacity for trivia.

"Triple A is going to catch on—all those broken-down heaps of junk needing a tow truck, one after the other. The same membership number ten times in a row." Jen shakes her head, her hair briskly riding her shoulders.

"You're awfully pessimistic about our cars," Tucker accuses her.

Jen's eyes narrow, so Rick jumps in to conjure up the amused dispatcher at Triple A finally getting the picture: Cars strewn across I-90 and I-80, the same three people hitching a ride to the next town. "We'll be famous in Triple A."

"By then we'll be in Cleveland," Tucker says.

"Stranded in Cleveland," Rick corrects him. "We'll have to buy a five hundred dollar car to get us home." Suddenly he feels inordinately happy. It is hard to explain. He doesn't have to explain. He slouches further into the couch and puts his hands behind his head. Let it rain.

"Maybe stranded. We'll cross that bridge later," Tucker says, lining up their dead beer bottles. "Tell you what: I'll come back for your graduation. You guys do Pomp and Circumstance and grab those diplomas while I scout out the first car."

"Bull. You missed Sissy's graduation from med school, not to mention Dad's retirement party," Rick reminds him.

"It's not like the rest of the family made it to those events," Tucker says.

"So come June you'll be here for our graduation?" Jen's eyes narrow again behind her glasses "We can count on that?"

"Wouldn't miss it for anything," Tucker says. "Boston is the first stop on the way to Cleveland." He holds up his hand to Rick for a high five. The slap feels good.

The rain has let up, so they take a long walk for wine and bread, stopping by Commonwealth's Used Books and Pete's Mountain for espressos. Rick and Tucker catch up on family gossip and old friends. They all need a nap. Back at the apartment, Rick senses an unaccustomed shyness in Jen when they make love—or maybe something else. But they drift off to sleep, ankles entwined as usual, his nose buried in her hair.

Later that evening, showered and almost fresh, Rick prepares his standby recipe for salmon steaks while Tucker mixes up a pitcher of Manhattans. Her hair swinging free and fine, Jen sets the table and even finds two old candles. They drop into their chairs, a trio of appetites. "A toast to our reunion," Tucker says, "and to meeting Jen."

After an assessment of Rick's culinary skills, Jen turns to Tucker. "So how much money do you figure we should leave with?"

"Money? Leave with?" Tucker is concentrating on opening the second good Bordeaux.

"To Cleveland," Jen says. "Ten one-hundred dollar bills should do it. Maybe five each."

"Oh. Cleveland," Rick says, wondering when she did those calculations. He steals a glance at Tucker who listens in amazement as Jen describes how they will pay for every car with one crisp hundred-dollar bill. "In fact, whoever buys the car should go off with only one hundred-dollar bill," Jen says. "That way no one will be tempted to pay a dollar more for any one car."

Rick sees Tucker trying to recall where plans for this Boston/Cleveland trip left off, but Tucker is tired and has an early flight tomorrow. They are all moderately drunk.

"Jen. Jen, baby, we can't go there," Tucker finally says, dipping his beard into his chest.

"What do you mean, 'baby'?" Jen says, her voice sharply sober.

Tucker's surprised look is a brief spark. Then, he shakes his head, "Nah. We've already made that trip."

"Made that trip?" Jen says, and Rick wonders which annoys her more: "Jen, baby" or the cancelled trip.

"We made that trip this afternoon," Tucker says. "I thought you caught on to us. All our family trips."

"Family trips?" Rick says. He doesn't remember one. And then belatedly he catches on: it is true, though he wishes it were not. Finally he adds, mournfully, for Jen's sake. "Tucker's right. That trip's behind us." He glances at Tucker who is nodding his head, regret softening his eyes, and suddenly they both begin to laugh, Tucker's beard dancing with a last show of energy.

"Hey Ricky, did you hear us?" Tucker sputters, wiping his eyes.

"Do we sound like Mom and Dad or what!" Rick says. He feels alarmed and guilty but he can't stop laughing.

Jen's puzzlement is giving way to anger. She peers at his desk, the couch, and Rick knows she is looking for a barrette to pin up her hair. Sure enough, its burnished length is soon pulled back and tightly coiled.

"You have to fill Jen in," Tucker says, starting to hiccough. "All those family vacations we planned. The rafting trip down Bright Angel Creek in the Grand Canyon. Fishing in Idaho. Skiing in Vail."

Rick continues the list—the non-vacations. "Those cooking lessons in Tuscany, Graceland. Oh, God, and the Shakespeare Festival in Toronto after you had the eighth grade lead in Romeo and Juliet." Rick balls up his napkin and throws it at Tucker. "The last trip we didn't take was to visit you in Ecuador. I had five different reservation codes with three different airlines before I let that one go."

"I bet you…never even got…to all those…those immunizations," Tucker howls and hiccoughs both.

"I misplaced the malaria pills after the first two days, you bastard. And luckily I only got through the first round of shots." Rick is gasping for air. Jesus, he has missed this laughter. He sneaks a look at Jen and sees that an explanation is needed. Now. "What my drunk brother is trying to say is that we never took one family vacation," Rick says. "We planned a million, but never took one."

Tucker sets his wine glass down so hard a little liquid spills. "Do you think it's possible our parents don't know?" Tucker says to Rick.

"They're probably planning something right this minute," Rick says.

Tucker turns to Jen. "So, there's no way we can go to Cleveland." Beginning to sputter again, he says, "Don't you see: that would…ruin… everything."

Jen doesn't see, or maybe refuses to. When she begins gathering up plates, Rick rises to help, asking who wants cognac or maybe coffee.

Over coffee, a subdued Tucker delivers a brief précis of the talk he'll be giving in Brazil, describes his new condo in Chicago and the book he is working on. "Hey, enough about me," he says, looking from Rick to Jen. "Fill me in on the wedding plans."

Jen looks stricken, her coffee mug motionless in front of her.

So Rick begins. Not looking at either of them, he tells Tucker about the ceremony they wrote a month ago, the country B&B they plan to rent for the entire September weekend. "We've got it all figured out," he says, not sure exactly when it all started. He pulls Jen's hand toward him and covers it with his own as he goes on to describe the Friday arrival dinner, Saturday morning's hike or golf game depending. Noon box lunch. The late afternoon wedding. Dinner and dancing under the stars. Brunch the next morning. The two-week honeymoon on Maui. "Now we just have to pin the family down on dates," he says.

Jen pulls her hand from under his—and Rick lets her. "We've already done the wedding," she says, rising from the table. "The actual wedding...would ruin everything." She picks up the coffee tray and turns as if to carry it to the kitchen. Then, cutting short this trip, she lets it drop. Cups shatter, sugar snows on the sorry landscape of Rick's floor. He stands as she gathers up her coat and purse and leaves. And then he sits back down.

"Smart woman," Tucker says.

Rick agrees. It is one of the reasons he once loved her.

Hindsight

CLARE AND HER OLDEST friend from college had been planning the visit for three months. But only yesterday, her arms full of towels and pillows, Clare realized that it was too soon for her husband's study to become a guest room. First, she needed to talk through her anguish and anger at finding him there, slumped over his desk beside the empty vials of pills, finding his folded note that said "Clare."

Today, Brenda was driving her rental car down from Maine, where she'd been camping with her youngest son and his girlfriend. The young couple was supposed to be staying behind in Castine for another week, so Clare was startled to see three people outside her back gate—Brenda, but also Brenda's son and a girl, looking irritable and unwashed.

She tried to hide her dismay as Brenda said "Oh, Clare," and folded her into strong arms. Nate hung back for a long moment, then stepped forward to introduce a shyly nodding Rebecca. The girl was runner-thin—noticeable in spite of the wrist-length sleeves of her Kinks t-shirt. She had long, red-blonde hair and red-rimmed eyes as if she'd gotten sun-screen in them, or had been crying. Nate's gangly arms and height mirrored his father's dark, messy good looks. Brenda's sunburned face was already peeling beneath her frown. Their car was crammed with backpacks and camping stuff, beach chairs, empty water bottles, soggy coffee cups, straw sun hats; the Volvo's engine—even off—sputtered in the humid August heat.

Clare ushered them past the patio's wilted ferns and roses into the cool house, where Brenda instructed Nate to pile everything in the mudroom to be sorted out later. When the kids trudged outside for more, a distraught Brenda apologized for appearing with the unexpected guests. "Nate broke up with her so their backpacking plans for Maine are out."

"And now?" It was all Clare could offer.

"Oh, Clare, I knew you'd be upset, which is why I didn't call. Rebecca wants to go home. I'll put them both on a plane in the morning." She groaned and dropped onto the couch. "This week has been hell. Black flies. Cold water. The kids breaking up." Her blotched face attested to her motherly anxieties and her ample figure to the appetites that tried to assuage them. Closing her eyes, she promised to say more when the kids left to dump the rental car. "Did you mention Bloody Marys?"

It was a drink Stewart had loathed, but Clare gratefully mixed up a pitcher—shades of dorm room Sundays. After college they had kept in touch. Brenda and Cabot moved to Seattle, writing of the surprise of a third son, and Clare and Stewart relaying their own surprise at not having children. Clare was absorbed by the demands of arts administration and her increased ministrations to Stewart. For a while, his position as a civil engineer specializing in bridge work had served him well—when he was deep in plans, calculating the statistics of tensions and stresses or working on elaborate digital models. Between projects, Stewart's bouts with depression became a larger and larger part of their marriage. Clare found herself obsessively buying season tickets to the theatre and Red Sox games, making travel plans to view yet another of the world's great bridges, the sixth-century Anji Bridge in Zhaoxian or the Ponte Vecchio in Florence. Stewart would explain to her the religious beliefs, the military conquests, or the march of technology that made them possible. Travel was out of the question when his depression grew more pronounced—days spent in bed and nights in constant weeping before he agreed to several month-long stays in the hospital. And then his suicide.

Brenda was the only friend Clare wanted to talk to, though they agreed that she should not come out for the memorial service, but later. She needed time alone with Brenda, to cry, to remember Stewart's virtues and complain about his faults, and to talk about her anger at being left. How long had he been rehearsing his final goodbye? Had he been wondering what to write as they talked of next year's opera festival in Santa Fe, or her brother's knee operation? Had he lain beside her at night, perhaps after making love in their practiced and satisfying way, unable to sleep, composing his letter?

My Dearest Clare,

Please believe me that I've stayed as long as I could—for you. You, our life together kept me here longer than anything else could have. Don't look for signs in hindsight because there won't be any. I have to leave.

All my love,

Stewart

It was too courtly, infuriating in its reticence. How dare he claim full responsibility for his decision to end his life. Making it his story. Leaving her with what? Maybe she'd driven him to it in some way he did not want her to discover. If only—if only what? If only he'd loved her more?

She carried Bloody Marys and a pitcher of refills out to Brenda, who was fanning herself with a magazine on the patio. As the sun slipped from the high brick walls, the afternoon had grown blessedly cooler, so they sat amidst the geraniums and ivy on rusting iron chairs, aware that any minute, Nate and Rebecca would be back from dropping off the car.

"Tell me fast what happened with the kids," Clare said.

Brenda glanced at her watch, then began by saying that soon after Nate and Rebecca started dating he discovered she was into cutting. "Little nicks to draw blood. Or pin pricks. When he learned she was bulimic, he was already in love and desperate for her to see a therapist, afraid she might commit suicide." She stopped short—"Oh,

Clare"—and leaned forward to touch Clare's arm.

Clare shook her head, willing herself not to cry. "Go on," she said. "It's OK. No, it's not OK, but you know what I mean."

Brenda's eyes searched Clare's for just that meaning.

"Please go on," she said.

The patio gate squeaked. Brenda held out her glass for a refill. "Ice is heaven," she said. The kids were back.

They couldn't go to Clare's favorite restaurant because Rebecca was a vegan. A bulimic vegan. Clare didn't want to think about Rebecca's tastes—any of them, going down or coming up. Dinner conversation was sparse, awkward, and Clare noted with sadness that Rebecca's fork was empty half the time it rose from her plate. Walking home after dinner, Nate and Rebecca seemed desperate to be with someone other than themselves. Nate told Clare more than she ever wanted to know about landscaping. How soil had its own form of DNA, that pedestrians' muddy shortcuts were called "desire lines." Rebecca walked silently beside Brenda, occasionally looking over her shoulder at Clare and Nate. When Brenda asked about school, snippets of Rebecca's talk about her courses floated back—the politics of gender, her class on iconic architecture.

Back home, in a waif-like voice that unexpectedly pierced Clare's heart, Rebecca said she'd like to turn in early, so Clare gathered up sheets and a pillow for the living room couch upstairs. She wanted to shake Rebecca or take her in her arms and say, "You have a whole life ahead of you," but it was something she wasn't quite convinced of for herself. Rebecca's curved back, her thin shoulders as she tucked in the sheets, looked too taut and fragile to touch. Her polite help with the pillowcase was painful. Clare left to find more pillows. Brenda would sleep in Stewart's study—it had become a "guest room" after all. Nate was given blankets for the couch in the family room downstairs, where Brenda and Clare were once again unable to talk.

Tomorrow, if they couldn't change their tickets, Clare would insist the kids go off somewhere—The MFA, the waterfront, Paul Revere's house—anywhere. She and Brenda deserved time off from the banal drama of this failed youthful romance.

Brenda had changed into a cotton flowered bathrobe and, feet up on the coffee table, balanced a mug of strong black tea on her stomach. Every so often Nate tilted his dark head toward the stairs as if to listen—for what, Clare wondered. His voice was thick as he relayed how Rebecca didn't believe he was serious that their relationship was over. He actually said *relationship*. "She keeps making plans for a bike trip we were going to do next summer." Then wistfully, "I think I'll go up and say good night. See how she is."

Please stay a while, Clare wanted to say.

Brenda rose to brew another cup of tea, then in a low voice, continued the story of Rebecca's life. That her father died when she was ten so they moved in with grandparents while her mother kept books for an auto body shop. Rebecca went to Barnard on a full scholarship, and Nate to Stanford, where his freshman year was consumed by long distance calls pleading with Rebecca to go for counseling. In the spring he gave her an ultimatum and she promised things would change. Then on this trip to Maine Nate said that tiny dots began appearing on her arms again. "She wore long-sleeved t-shirts the entire week in Maine, even though it was close to 100." Clare had noticed those long sleeves when they arrived. Who knew?

Brenda sighed. "Rebecca hasn't called home at all, not even when Nate told her it was over. This was Nate's first real romance. They don't realize that they'll get over it. He feels grief-stricken—" Brenda stopped.

Nate stumbled halfway down the spiral stairs to lean over the railing. "Mom, Rebecca said a strange thing. She said to come get her in the morning if she doesn't wake up."

"Why wouldn't she wake up?" Brenda asked, annoyance setting hard the corners of her mouth. "Do you want me to talk to her?"

"No, I'll go." Nate disappeared up the stairs only to reappear a moment later.

"Mom. Mom, I think you better come upstairs. Please. She took all her pills." He waved three pharmacy vials, their tops off, empty.

"Oh God," Brenda cried. Then she was up the stairs, holding her robe high, her glance back at Clare beseeching.

No, Clare thought. This cannot be happening. Rebecca's orange plastic vials were identical to those Stewart had saved up the last four months. Where had he kept his precious hoard of death?

Rebecca was bent over in a shroud of pale blue sheets on the edge of the couch, her thin arms holding her concave stomach. Clare had never seen arms that thin and helpless. Nate's arm around her shoulder looked too heavy for her to bear.

When Brenda asked if she'd taken all the pills, she nodded, eyes vacant and glazed.

"Up, up!" Brenda said, shaking Nate's shoulder "Get her to the bathroom, she has to vomit. Right, Clare?"

In a rerun of her call six months ago, Clare dialed 911, awash in anger that such questions hadn't been necessary when she came home to find Stewart slumped at his desk—his neck unearthly cold—his plans more sincerely made.

As calmly as she could—was her address in police records—Clare answered the dispatcher's questions and listened to instructions. "If she is throwing up, don't flush. They might want to see what's there." Next was what had she taken and how much.

Speaking over the wet sounds of Rebecca's retching, Clare read off the labels: "Lithium, Xanax, Tylenol. Nate, how much?" He was kneeling in front of the toilet beside a heaving Rebecca, holding back her straggly wet hair in one hand, her forehead in his other. He repeated Clare's question and Rebecca shook her head, unable or unwilling to say how many pills had gone down. When 911 asked how much was coming up Clare forced herself to look at the floating dinner, the revolting debris of wild mushroom risotto and partially digested pills. "Hard to tell," she said. Meanly, she couldn't help thinking that the bulimic Rebecca must find this part easy.

Then the 911 voice said, "If nothing more is coming up, get her walking and keep her walking."

Minutes later, paramedics came to the door, black bags in hand, stretcher ready. Rebecca's name and age?

"Lord, I don't know." Helplessly, Clare turned to Nate, who was walking a limp Rebecca around and around the living room. Her thin white nightgown hung on the sharply flat body of a child. Poor Rebecca surely didn't know Clare's name either. She must feel so alone with her shredded heart.

The paramedics walked her out, one on each side of her. "Better to walk," they said. Was there a note? No note, Clare said, thinking that a gesture doesn't require a note. Brenda was the last through the door. "I shouldn't leave you," Brenda said, but she was moving down the stairs.

"Go," Clare said. "Go." She flushed the toilet twice, wiped down the seat, and threw Rebecca's sheets into the laundry. She tried to keep at bay unbidden images of Stewart being taken away on a stretcher, his face covered shockingly in a shiny body bag, no longer an emergency. In that way, except for his note, he simply disappeared. In the weeks that followed she became obsessed with knowing what it meant. She'd found accounts of a note carried in a locket where once a picture had been; a note torn in two by a sister who wanted to keep a father's dire prediction about a younger brother secret from him; another thrown away by a cousin who only valued stock certificates. Then there were the notes of Virginia Woolf, Rudolph Hess, Yukio Mishima, Kurt Cobain, and books of collected suicide notes: the improbable *To Be or Not To Be* and *I'm In the Tub, Gone. Let Me Finish* was a Christmas best-seller in Germany. One suicide note said "I'm annoyed that I will miss the O.J. Simpson trial." And another was a list that ended "Buy eggs; Shoot Sam [the cat], Shoot self." Was a note better than no note? Some experts said that suicide runs in families, though whether it was psychological or something genetics didn't yet understand wasn't clear. For several months after Stewart's death, Clare had regretted that they hadn't had a child, but would she ever have stopped worrying about her child's future when her own husband had been such a tenuous guest on this earth?

The emergency room entrance of Mt. Auburn Hospital bristled and glowed with the lights of three parked ambulances, as policemen directed yet another siren's arrival. In the waiting room, Brenda wept and blew her nose, saying this must bring it all back for Clare. No, Clare thought. It was never really gone. Down the hall, Nate hovered outside Rebecca's bay and from time to time went to the cafeteria for coffees. They called Rebecca's mother, but she wasn't home. An hour later, Doctors assured them that the charcoal had worked, that Rebecca would recover just fine. If she had walked in at that moment, her white hospital gown dragging on the tiled floor, Clare would have slapped her silly.

Exhausted, they went home at four a.m. and slept till eight. After checking in with the hospital, Clare suggested she make omelets while Brenda tried to reach Rebecca's mother again. "I almost don't know where to begin," Brenda said, and Clare told her, "Just dial."

When Brenda returned, Clare set her to grating a sharp cheddar. It disappeared in short furious strokes as Brenda said, "You're not going to believe this, Clare, but after everything I described her mother said, 'I suppose I should send flowers.'" She stopped grating, clearly expecting an equally appalled reaction from Clare, who instead yanked the grater out of her hands and clunked it into the sink. "That poor woman is probably in shock." Her voice was too harsh, even to her own ears. "It's not yet six a.m. in Seattle. We didn't think of that."

A chastised Brenda rinsed the grater automatically and dried it. "I told her that what she needed to do was make plane reservations. She's probably totally baffled by Rebecca."

"And maybe I'm still baffled by Stewart's death," Clare said. Why, why hadn't she been a strong enough force to keep him here? He had known that would be her question: Don't look for signs in hindsight. Damn Stewart. That is not an answer.

"Oh, Clare, I am so sorry for all of this."

"Brenda, look at me. What is 'all of this'?"

"Everything. These last few horrible days. Stewart."

"We haven't even talked of Stewart," Clare said. She turned the heat to high.

"But at least you understand what made him do it. His difficult last years," Brenda said, putting her hands on Clare's trembling shoulders.

"Is that what you think? That I understand. You're relieved that I understand?" She pulled free of Brenda to splash whipped eggs into the hot skillet. How could Brenda have arrived at this point? There had been no bridge to here, no arc from one side to the other.

"That came out wrong," Brenda said.

"What I want to know is why I'm so fucking angry," Clare said. "Go home."

Brenda's shocked look was far more satisfying than her sympathy.

"You heard correctly," Clare said. "Not sad. Not heart-broken. Yes, that. But angry, too."

"Dear Clare." Clumsily, Brenda pulled the skillet from Clare's hand, and slid it off the burner. "His note, I'd hoped—"

"Maybe it was the best he could do," Clare said. And maybe the best she could do was make all these false starts—talk and hope for some coherent story to emerge that would pull it all together. "I'm sorry. Please don't go," she told Brenda. Not yet.

The next day, Clare sat outside the state mental hospital in Newton, waiting for Brenda and Nate. They'd brought Rebecca magazines and books, a bouquet of irises. Massachusetts State Law dictates that anyone who attempts suicide must go through evaluation before being released, so Rebecca had been delivered by ambulance to a facility locked-down floor by floor. Their visit had been difficult to arrange because they weren't family. When Rebecca's mother called to say she'd be here by the weekend, Clare pictured her getting on a plane for the first time and flying east, her eyes closed the entire way. She'd get a cab to the hospital, bewildered by Boston's one-way streets and the unfamiliar grid of suburbs. Clare probably should offer her a place to stay, but she simply could not do it. The hospital would have lists of nearby hotels and B&Bs. Brenda and Nate were leaving tomorrow. Nate had resisted, but, wisely, Brenda had persuaded him to go home. His summer job was waiting. Friends. His own life. And Clare insisted that Brenda go with him. "He needs you," she said.

In truth, Clare wanted to be done with all of them. She felt drained of sympathy, almost inhuman. And now this final goodbye to Rebecca was taking longer than expected. She craned her neck to look at the depressing row of barred fifth-floor windows. All this could have been me, she thought, driving back and forth to Newton. Bringing the daily crossword to Stewart; buying biographies for Stewart; planning a trip to see the Rockville Bridge in Pennsylvania, one of the world's most beautiful structures. Or the Akashi Kaikyo Bridge in Japan. The Mackinac Bridge in upper Michigan. She would have been desperate to anchor Stewart in the world—to be his anchor—to search for literally what would make him care enough to stay alive.

The sharp tap on the window startled her before a depleted Brenda sank into the passenger's seat. Nate's eyes were red, his shoulder wet.

"The doctors say she'll be able to return to school in a month," Brenda said. "I don't know how well they understand the situation— the pressure of Barnard, her clueless mother. But they'll meet her soon enough."

"Yes," Clare said. She hadn't seen Rebecca since the paramedics walked her to the ambulance. It was unlikely she'd ever see her again. She'd already forgotten Rebecca's last name. It was all dissonance. Her head ached.

Behind them, Nate was rummaging in his backpack. Moments later, he was on his cell phone with a friend, his recounting of the events of the past two days impossible to ignore. His voice quavered with excited grief as he relayed details of the drama—their break-up, her pills, the wavering Rebecca walking, walking. He should have known, he said. How had he put it together so quickly? Clare wondered. Become the center of the story. This kid.

She tried to tune him out.

His cell phone snapped shut. "Mom, I really should stay till her mother comes, explain about breaking up."

Clare's exasperation flooded the car as she burst out, "Nate. It wasn't your fault. What is wrong with Rebecca is beyond what you can do." She pulled too sharply into traffic. Horns blared.

"But who's going to tell her mother what happened?"

"The doctors," Brenda said, but her voice lacked conviction.

Clare dreaded the next few hours. "You don't really know what happened," she said.

But clearly he thought he did, because he was punching a new number into the phone. "You're not going to believe…"

"Stop. Enough," Clare yelled. She swerved to the curb, just missing the fender of a black Mercedes, and pulled hard on the brake. Brenda's hands flew to the dash, her shoulders rounded high with fear. Nate clicked shut his phone.

Searching his surprised, hurt gaze in the rear view, Clare said she refused to be a party to the next ten calls he was going to make between Newton and Boston. "Can you please wait until we get home? Can you please give Rebecca some privacy?"

That evening, Brenda was shy with Clare, wary, but they got through the awkward dinner and retired early. Only after the taxi was called the next morning did Clare and Brenda grow misty-eyed, thick-throated as they made plans for another visit.

"We never talked about Stewart," Brenda said. "It's what I came for."

"You'll come back soon," Clare said. "And I will still be here."

Then they were gone.

Methodically, she collected towels and sheets, straightened chairs, restoring each room to its normal use. In Stewart's study, she put the folding bed away, removed the vase of wilted flowers, the tray of toiletries on his desk. Then she stood in the doorway, remembering that lonely, lousy night six months ago, the day of Stewart's death. After friends and neighbors left, she gathered up coffee cups and wine glasses, and carried them to the kitchen, where she'd poured a glass of his favorite single malt. She recalled how its smell of peat and Scotland left her trembling with grief. Then she took Stewart's note to his study, certain of what she needed to do: retrace his last moments before he'd swallowed his pills.

She sat where he'd sat—in his old leather swivel chair at his rosewood desk. Sipping from his favorite glass, she forced herself to imagine his last movements, his folded arms, his sloping shoulders, his lowered head. Oh, Stewart, why?

She leaned back in his chair to be him. She felt his intent expand her rib cage, she felt his urgency push against her heart. His Namiki Vanishing Point fountain pen still rested on his desk. The empty pharmacy vials were an orange cluster, and a fine white powder still dusted the old-fashioned green blotter where he had scattered the pills. An empty water glass had been pushed toward the lamp. He had folded the note once and written "Clare." His handwriting was steady, precise, so he must have worn his reading glasses.

Now, standing in this doorway months later, she understood what he'd done—unable to stay, Stewart had left her behind. She was alone with what he had given her—and taken away. This was her story. Eyes closed, Clare watched him take off his glasses as she'd watched a thousand times before. Finally, he had cupped the pills in the palm of his hand. He'd lifted the glass, and then—as simple or as complex as that—he'd swallowed their life.

Empty Summer Houses

DAVID'S WIFE, HER BLONDE ponytail swaying above her jacket, her boots crunching on oyster shells, had turned off the sandy lane onto the white path that led to the house she'd added to her List in August. Three weeks ago, after they'd photographed an improbably pink stucco McMansion on the bay, he'd decided that stalking empty summer houses was getting too strange—not what they saw, but doing it. Today, he'd promised himself, was the last time. After this, Liz was on her own. He hadn't told her yet. But he would.

"David, see that," Liz said. She pointed to a limp garden hose and a wheelbarrow propped against a dilapidated shed with no door. "Eerie, right?"

Ignoring "eerie," David said, "Why didn't they just put the gardening stuff in the shed?" "Eerie" was Liz's major criterion for the photographs she'd taken for the past two years: broken lawn chairs, rocks collected on beach walks, silvery chunks of driftwood. Then through their windows: crooked lamp shades, couches swathed in sheets, paintings of watery landscapes and molten sunsets, a red kayak in the middle of a living room floor, wind chimes on a table, kids' stuffed animals. To David, these houses just looked neglected, empty.

"I'll leave the shed for later," Liz said, patting the camera he'd given her last year for her thirtieth birthday. Her ponytail beckoned him onward.

"Fine," David said.

It was November and most of the summer houses in this Outer Cape town had been closed up for the winter. Water drained, deck furniture dragged inside, plywood nailed over windows facing ocean or bay as the population went from 65,000 to 4,000 in a matter of days. Traffic disappeared and cloth-napkin restaurants closed. The back roads of Truro and Wellfleet were hidden and lush in summer, but fall pulled down their curtains of leaves and vines, and houses of wildly varying proportions and styles seemed to appear overnight. Many summer residents were now the proud, though absentee, owners of what was called in real estate parlance "a winter water view."

David stopped to assess the compact one-story house ahead, caged in by tall, scraggly pines. A spongy carpet of needles rimmed the path to the front door and dry leaves ruffled the edges of the gray shingled walls. Everything gray. Cedar roof, decks. Gray. Mortal.

They'd started photographing empty houses the autumn after Rosie died. She was four months old, when late one June night she stopped breathing. The ambulance's siren split their world in two. The next day they were childless. Soiled diapers still reeked in the pail; the mobile of circus animals still trembled above Rosie's crib. David found himself clasping a throw pillow against his chest. Liz was inconsolable. That fall, her breasts dry and the baby furniture stored in the attic, they took long walks to get out of the house. Liz began to keep a list of odd, closed-up houses to photograph. She called her collection Empty Summer Houses. If she ever displayed them, which he suspected she would do sometime in the future—maybe in her next Provincetown show—it would be a form of transgressive art.

This morning she'd said, "OK. Let's take a walk. I want to visit the house set back from Balston Beach." It was her way of getting them past the argument they'd had last night. David had started it by saying let's think about having a child. Liz had slammed down her wine glass so hard the stem broke. "How can you say that without adding the word 'another'? Have you forgotten her?" she cried. And he'd said, "Never. But I want to raise a child. I don't want to replace Rosie. I want a different child. Children." Turning away, she said what she always said, that it was too soon. This time he'd countered with, "Then when? It's been two years. We don't have one photograph of Rosie anywhere." He'd never pushed so hard before. Last week in the

Stop and Shop, in line behind a harried father with a squalling baby, the smell of Johnson's Baby Powder nearly made him cry. "When?" She'd slept in the guest room.

After a silent breakfast, she'd thrown his barn coat at him and said, "Come on." He'd hesitated—long enough for Liz to ask "what?"—so he put on his coat, telling himself this was his last such walk.

Having declared that the shed was for later, Liz led them to where they were now—peering through the screens of a large porch, so open that it was the obvious place to start. The Cape hadn't had a first snow, but when it did, everything on the porch would be covered in a sifting of white.

They pressed their noses to separate panels, inhaling the fall screen smell, metallic and woodsy. The porch had the sort of clutter that David had come to admire, even envy. A round Weber grill missing its lid and filled with pillows of gray ash stood beside a statue of a cement cupid holding cement grapes. In the corner, a dimpled soccer ball. A second green hose, newer, wound around and through various wicker chairs and small wrought-iron tables. An old glider reminded him of the one his grandmother once had, gently sliding back and forth, a movement a swing could never replicate.

Liz took two or three dozen photos. Two trellises leaning against a wall had caught her eye. Dry bits of vines still twisted in and out of the squares. She'd always liked squares, checks, polka dots, clay roof tiles on Italian villas, twenty nude torsos of mannequins in the window of a store going out of business—all patterns. He could have predicted her choice for Rosie's wallpaper—tiny pink rosebuds that, from a short distance, looked not like rosebuds, but delicate splashes of color. Gone. Stripped away a month later.

Lagging behind, David photographed the cupid and red tricycle. The cupid's concrete arms and legs and tummy were all soft gray curves. The tricycle's seat was cracked and crooked. He pictured Rosie's bruised knee and a faded blue tennis shoe doing a left dismount. He longed to pinch the bell and hear its fuzzy ring. Rosie always waved her chubby arms when they set her mobile into musical motion.

"David," Liz called. He hurried to catch up.

Methodically, they began to circle the house, looking in every ground floor window that had an interior view. Flimsy curtains covered the windows of the first two narrow rooms—probably bunk rooms for kids—but not the kitchen's. It was circa 1950 with stainless steel counters and a fridge with a rounded top.

Liz pointed to the rotisserie standing on its splayed four legs. "Just like my mother's," she said. Her camera's shutter clicked four times.

To David, it looked like a baby's bassinet, but he didn't say so. A row of seven coffee pots on a top shelf attested to not much being given away—or moving on to the swap area at the Wellfleet dump. "Dump"—a word the woman at town hall still used, to David's joy, when he got their yearly "Transfer Station" sticker.

"Now, there's a shot," Liz said.

He strained to see what she was seeing. "That space under the sink?" he ventured. A limp curtain covered with perky chickens hatching eggs was pushed to one side, revealing all the household poisons: Lysol, Fantastic, Clorox, Windex, Murphy's Oil Soap. Enough to kill a houseful of kids. What would Liz title it? Rather, why?

As she focused on the lethal collection of cleaning solutions, he moved to the next window and peered into a pantry or mudroom. Two dolls stared from the seat of an old wooden highchair, the counters were piled high with stainless mixing bowls and a bottle warmer. The floor was cluttered with sand toys—plastic pails and shovels, a water mill he would have loved. It wouldn't do for Liz, but he'd loop back after she moved on. His thoughts snagged on those words "moved on" and brought back last night's argument. Could he ever stand to be without her? Here, they were known as year-rounders, both teachers at the Truro high school, where he used to think he taught teenagers, but now he thought of them with affection as somebody's children. As kids themselves, they both had looked forward to a month's summer vacation on the Cape where they stayed in the tiny stand-alone cabins like delicate dolls' houses lining the long shore road to Provincetown. Perched just five to twenty feet from the azure bay depending on the tide, they all had flower names: Petunia, Goldenrod, Wisteria, Lily. As teenagers, they fell in love with the Cape, and then with each other while working hot summers as fry cooks at The Lobster Pot in Provincetown. Their clothes reeked of oil and both sets of parents insisted they undress outside their cabins. Giggling, they had run into the shimmering surf, declaring this is where they wanted to raise a family. Or was.

"You'll want to skip the pantry," he called out, feeling sad and also mean. Withholding from her the beautifully carved highchair. He rounded a corner, ankle deep in brown leaves. And then he saw it. A narrow wooden door ten feet away, open about an inch, and probably leading to a washing machine or hot water heater. The wind must have done that. "Liz," he called. "Come see."

He slowly pulled on the metal handle and the door scraped open about a foot.

In this moment, more than anything, he wanted to go through that door. "Liz," he called again. He needed to push her through into some unknown space.

When she came around the corner, her eyebrows raised in a question, he pulled her forward to stand in front of him. "Our lucky day," he said, and reached around her to tug the door open all the way. Then he firmly placed his hands on her shoulders and propelled her through. She swung around as if to hit him, then stumbled and turned so she wouldn't fall as he continued to push her forward through this narrow damp room and into the kitchen.

"Jesus, David," she said. "Are you crazy? Now we're trespassing." Her nose was red. Her ponytail swung in wide, angry arcs.

"We're not doing any harm," he said, shivering. "What? Are the police going to show up?" It was colder in the house than it had been outside. He took his hands from her shoulders to bury them in his pockets.

"You know Charlie does rounds on all the empty houses," she said, peeling back a curtain to peer through the dusty window above the sink.

"Like our friend is going to pull out his handcuffs. Like he's not going to buy our neighborly story about looking after our neighbor's summer place."

Liz swished the curtain down. "Neighbors whose name we don't know." She moved as if to leave but he caught her arm.

"Just this once," he said. "You can't see everything from the outside." He pointed to a meager collection of salt and pepper shakers on a narrow shelf above the stove—all cutely brazen animals. Then to a potholder with a seriously burned corner.

"Five minutes," Liz said, jerking free. Unable to resist, she raised her camera to take six photographs of the poisons under the sink. Then the kitchen sink itself.

He left her and walked into the next room, a sort of parlor. White bookshelves were filled with National Geographics and mostly smart people's books: Hillary Mantel, Robert Caro, Cees Nooteboom, Witold Rybczynski, John Banville, Murakami, Bolaño, Krugman, Tolstoy. No mysteries. No "summer books." Every book bristled with a bookmark and was dog-eared, as if the reader in the house stopped before the end of each story. Surely it wasn't possible that someone could live with all these unknown endings.

He called out for Liz to join him. "Only another minute," he promised when she appeared. As she scanned the shelves, he said "Notice that every book has a dog-eared page also marked with a bookmark."

When Liz pulled *Anna Karenina* off the shelf, it fell open on its own.

"Maybe we should leave a note, explaining how each story ends?" he said. "We want you to know that Anna (after page 224) leaves her husband of the big ears and her beloved young son for Vronsky who turns out to be a cad, which leads Anna to commit suicide."

"She wanted to change her mind in those last moments," Liz said.

He said he didn't remember it that way.

He pulled out *Dune*, one of his favorite books, and put it back. "But why did they stop reading?" he wanted to know. "All these unfinished books frozen in place."

As if to ignore what he'd just said, or to confound the house's incurious readers, with a grandiose gesture Liz plucked out the bookmarks from one entire shelf and stuffed them into her windbreaker's pocket.

"Don't," he said.

She took more photographs. "Don't what?" she said. She took more bookmarks. "You brought me here."

"That's all I did." David retraced his steps to the mudroom to make sure he'd closed the door behind them. Returning, he stumbled over a single two-by-four propped just inside the doorframe. He dragged it over to a tiny window to see it in the light.

On the first four-inch side, unevenly-spaced horizontal lines rose from the bottom. Each line had a name and a number: Sam, age two, age three, four, five, six, up to ten, and each age was accompanied by a date. Sam was ten and tall this past summer. Slowly David turned the two-by-four. Ben's side was next. He was now eight. Zoe's narrower side was next. She was four last summer. David pictured their father holding them still, his hand on their rounded tummies, then using a ruler and pencil to mark how much they had grown in the past year. Each kid would step away, eager to see their progress. It was evidence of a real summer family—now a winter family somewhere else.

"David. David. Where are you?" Liz's voice rang out. And then she was there, her gaze sweeping up and down the two-by-four, asking what he was holding in his hand.

"A family record," he said. "Here, read it." He toppled it toward her and she was forced to catch it.

"Sam," she read, "age ten," and stricken, stopped.

"And Ben and Zoe," David said, pointing to the penciled lines. "Look how fast they're growing."

"Where did you find this?" Liz said, her voice breaking. "We need to leave. Charlie doesn't need to be put to the test."

But the test was for himself. His heart was forever gone from this venture. "Liz, Liz," he said, taking the two-by-four from her, leaning it back in place. "When we're out here photographing other people's houses, our own house is empty." He turned her around and gathered her into his arms, her boxy camera a dark and silent heart between them.

She closed her eyes.

"I won't do this again," he said.

"Don't leave me," she said against his chest. The camera had to be hurting her as it was hurting him. He held her tighter for now.

Prodigal Sister

MERRILL, THE MIDDLE SISTER and last to arrive, stood on one side of her father's hospital bed, Dora and Pip on the other. It was the old alignment of two against one and Merrill, even in her grief, found it as disconcerting as ever. Their father lay before them, as though the white sheet were an enormous weight, his breathing a courtesy—or curse— of the oxygen unit connected by pale blue tubes to his pinched nose. His gray hair seemed finely dusted onto his mottled scalp. She leaned forward to take her father's cold, diminished hand. "Dad, it's Merrill, I'm back to—back for another conference." It was a weak lie in the face of the unaccustomed presence of all three daughters. His paper-thin eyelids quivered, maybe.

"He knows why we're here," Pip said.

"Hush," Dora said, but she put her plump arm around Pip's narrow waist. Sadly, Dora looked older than her thirty-nine years, and Pip younger than thirty-one. Merrill was exactly in the middle. "Merrill in the middle" had been one of her sisters' infuriating childhood chants, casting her even further outside their childish sphere.

Moments earlier, Dora had solemnly greeted Merrill in the ICU hallway of Mass General, one of the medical meccas of the world, where people still, though not unaccountably, died. In a hushed, dramatic voice, she had relayed to Merrill the nurse's warning—surely the nurse meant it merely as information—that being in a coma did not exempt their father from overhearing what was said. "I wish she hadn't told us that," Dora said. "Pip has this idea that we should—that we need to confront him."

Now, in a practiced gesture, Dora swabbed their father's cracked lips with ice as Merrill looked for a place to put her coat and purse. There was nothing of their father in this sterile ICU room—no fraying books, eyeglasses, chewed pencils. One brown fake-leather recliner loomed in a corner, heavy with doom. The room reeked of disinfectant but somehow it still felt—unclean. There were no flowers, though once their father had taken such pride in their mother's garden, its profuse growth of sunflowers and begonias and lilies taller than her daughters. Merrill would bring flowers tomorrow.

Six months before, when she'd come to Boston for a conference, she'd nagged him about his teetering piles of books, knee-high beside every chair, nose-high on every table. As a professor of history he'd always seemed to inhabit an earlier time, an age without bookshelves. Merrill pictured him as St. Jerome at his table, a skull lurking on the windowsill beside a bored cat. And surely he wasn't eating right, given the large number of Dinty Moore Beef Stew cans and Lorna Doone cookie boxes in the trash. He'd nagged her in turn about her single status—making a dismissive gesture with his hand when she reminded him that it was historically accurate to say that her two sisters were also single, in view of their respective divorces—that they were all single. "Oh history," he'd said, and to her chagrin, dismissed that too.

Now, beneath the sheet that already resembled a shroud, his lips slack, he seemed incapable of dismissing anything. How can a heart bear such ambivalence to grief as Merrill's heart now beat—suspecting what was coming. In the past two years, each sister had passed on to Merrill what the other sister said. Pip was the first to call, saying "I heard from Dora last night." Merrill assumed that Dora's news, relayed through Pip, would be about her divorce and the complicated dissolution of financial ties. "That's not why Dora called," Pip said, her voice a whisper. "Dora called to talk about Dad. She says it started two years after Mom died."

Merrill recalled asking what had started. She'd been quietly paging through a catalogue of camping equipment—fold-up stoves, iodine filters, mosquito nets.

"Dad," Pip said. "Going into Dora's room. At night."

"No." Merrill slapped shut the catalogue. "What are you talking about? Do you know what you're saying?"

Pip said, "She'll tell you about it herself when she's ready," and then she hung up.

Merrill had waited for Dora's call, her disbelief and apprehension building, but Dora's call was not about Dora, it was about Pip. "Did you know Pip has been seeing a therapist for the past month?" Dora asked, gratified that no, Merrill had not known. Dora went on to say that Pip had started therapy after Dora's revelation had caused repressed memories of their father entering her room to come flooding back. How he carefully closed the door behind him, his silhouette becoming one with that closed door. "Do you remember," Dora asked Merrill, "when Dad stopped calling Pip 'Pipsqueak'? Did you ever wonder why?"

Unspoken in both calls was Merrill's part of the story. And neither sister asked.

The sisters were probably talking about Merrill now on their trip to the cafeteria for coffee.

Still standing by her father's bed, she whispered, "Dad," to his shrunken eyes. "Can you hear me?" She remembered her mother's final exhausted days, and then at their mother's gravesite, how their father said that nothing, nothing ever prepared you for the awful, mysterious arrival of death. "Here one moment, then gone," he'd said.

"You're still here," Merrill told him now, "I love you and you have loved me well. That history will not change." The morphine drip was surely a river of love and lies, and what he needed now.

Exhausted from the plane trip, she fell into the recliner, the arms waxy under the push she gave them to settle back. She felt her sisters waiting. It was probably why they had arrived a day earlier—to talk, to plot, really, because Merrill knew what her sisters wanted: they wanted her to give voice to what they took for granted to be true. Merrill's part of the story.

That evening, they left the hospital close to eight, after a brief conference with doctors and nurses, whose calm observations and hopeless predictions made Merrill's heart flutter with dread. She feared not knowing what Pip and Dora were thinking as they all heard that their father would not live more than a few days.

The September evening could not dispel the day's dank humidity, but Merrill welcomed it after a day spent in the air-conditioned hospital. Their cab crept down Charles Street, then past the Public Gardens where swan boats were docked for the night, while actual swans nested safe in cages on the pond's tiny island. The bronze Make-Way-for-Ducklings pattered, web-footed, in a cheery row, replenished after each random act of vandalism. Where were those missing, separated ducklings now?

When they arrived at their hotel, Merrill was annoyed and vaguely hurt that her sisters had already settled into one room together. She would have the second bedroom—across the quasi-living room with a stage-set bar and three barstools—to herself. Staying at their father's small apartment had never been a possibility.

Dora showed Merrill around. A slim computer glowed on her nightstand, no doubt bristling with emails about esoteric subjects and Dora's latest essay on eighteenth century travel chronicles by women. Three dresses, one too appropriately black, were hanging in the closet, testament that she was not losing weight. Pip's dresses were half the size. Three novels were piled on Pip's bedside table, as if she'd not find a bookstore in all of Boston in the next few days, weeks? It was true that most were gone, and their father had lamented the demise of Victor Hugo, a guard cat in its window. Pip had draped paisley scarves over two sitting chairs, bought fresh flowers—but not for their father. How long would they be here? Merrill imagined Pip deciding what to bring to impose beauty—perhaps order—on their lives. She traveled with her shawls even when she visited Merrill, which wasn't often. Merrill was always surprised—and again hurt—when she learned how frequently Dora and Pip spent vacations together, traded gossip and recipes as they talked on the phone. As they were talking now in hushed voices while Merrill unpacked and washed her grieving face.

•

During dinner, they caught up on recent happenings: Dora's messy move to Cincinnati and her appointment as an associate professor in the English Department—a move that also triggered her divorce. Merrill surprised herself by thinking that Dora had always been good at leaving. Picking cat hair off her sweater, Pip recounted her search for a new condo welcoming to pets—her three Maine Coon cats—and an occasional lone visitor from her thriving cat hospital. When it was Merrill's turn, she described her disappointing new position with the Peace Corps, saying it was as corporate as IBM. She hurried over the details of her latest failed relationship, since they'd never even heard his name. Throughout, Merrill recognized the presence of something unspoken hanging in the air, the staticky atmosphere reminiscent of family gatherings with husbands soon to be cut loose—before secrets had been shared, Merrill realized now. When had they last been together? It must have been two Thanksgivings ago, when Dora roasted turkey breasts instead of the whole, heavy bird.

Sure enough, Dora suggested they forego after-dinner coffee. "We can't talk here."

Merrill wanted her coffee. "Aren't we talking now?"

"We started last night." Pip caught their waiter's eye for the bill. "Though we probably should have waited..."

"So, out with last night," Merrill said, and couldn't believe she'd said it, invited them to speak. Her cheeks flared with what she really wanted to say: no, let's end it here. He's dying. He's as good as dead. Can't it all die with him? But both sisters refused to say more. Merrill considered staying behind, ordering a cognac, but Dora's stolid insistence and Pip's thin, stricken face compelled her to return with them to their hotel. Merrill brushed her teeth, holding her own gaze steady in the mirror, practicing.

Ten minutes later they reconvened in the shared living room, in robes and pajamas, fuzzy slippers reminiscent of their teenage years.

"OK, you two, what will it be," Merrill said, bending over the tiny bar, rummaging through miniature bottles for the appropriate and necessary nightcaps.

"For Dad. Can we please just say 'cheers'?" she said, raising her glass.

But Dora was too busy arranging herself in the large overstuffed chair. Pip too ignored Merrill's feeble toast and sank into the couch, a novel held to her chest like a religious artifact. Merrill didn't want to know the book's title—to render it fraught with meaning. Still standing, she was afraid to land; everywhere felt like a corner. She went to the bar for more ice. Maybe more scotch. Finally, Pip said she'd begin because she seemed to be the one who needed to say something. "I want Dad to know that it isn't three separate dirty secrets any longer."

Three. Three felt like a sword plunged into Merrill's solid grief. It drove her to the couch, to sink into something. Because once again they weren't waiting to hear from her. Nothing had changed. They'd always talked across her, the two of them, as if across a body of water, incurious as to how deep or mysterious or even shallow it might be.

"Pip thinks we should say something to Dad," Dora said, smoothing the flannel neckline of her gown. "Though I think it's a bit late for that."

"I need to say something—just like I will eventually need to throw rotten eggs at his tombstone." Pip's laugh was ragged and brief, her book still in place. "If we get him a tombstone."

Merrill cried "Stop," she had to stop this charade. "Didn't you ever wonder why I was the one who remembered Dad's birthday, went home on holidays, helped Dad move to his apartment. Why I never said anything?"

"You always were like that," Dora said, looking not at Merrill but at Pip.

"Look at me. Like what?" Merrill cried.

"Listen to you."

"Dora, Pip. You have to know. It didn't happen to me."

Their faces hardened into lines that would soon see them into middle-age. "That isn't possible," Dora said.

"She's lying," Pip said. Then to Merrill, "Liar. I'd like to slap you."

"For what?" Merrill said "I can't make up something that—"

"Let her be, it will come back soon enough," Dora said. She snapped off the light on the table next to her.

"Could I please speak for myself?" Merrill said. "And maybe I'm not the one who's imagining, or I guess the word is 'recovering' events. People make false accusations about—"

Pip took hold of Merrill's wrists and yanked her out of the couch. "Surely the details were the same for you as they were for me and Dora. Come on, think back." Her eyes raked Merrill's face. In a shaking voice, Pip recalled for them his shadow in the doorway, his deep, rough voice creating secrets, and here Pip's voice cracked to say "his rough, gentle hands." Tears flying, Pip shook Merrill's wrists. Her hands felt raised in supplication. "Jesus fucking Christ, Merrill, before he came to bed he shaved for us."

"But not to me," Merrill whispered. "Not to me."

"You're lying." She dropped Merrill's wrists in fierce disgust.

Merrill reached for her glass to cool her burning forehead. "Get over it."

"Enough, Pip. We all need to get some sleep. And Merrill needs to sleep on it." Dora's voice wavered. "You and I slept on it for years."

Pip turned on a dime, and pointed a finger at Dora. "There's something else I need to say. You left us with him. You abandoned us."

Us? Merrill thought. When had she and Pip become "us?" It felt new, almost exhilarating, that "us," but it came at Dora's expense.

"Oh, Pip. I left for college, I didn't abandon you."

"You fled," Pip said.

"I'll never forgive myself for that," Dora said. "You're right. I did nothing. Said nothing."

"We need to get past that," Pip said. "Tonight. Not tomorrow. Tonight."

"Oh, baby," Dora said, taking Pip in her arms. "My poor baby. OK. Let's talk."

For the next hour, Dora and Pip, their backs propped against the headboard of Pip's bed, told Merrill their separate stories—stories almost the same. The same night visits. The smell of aftershave Dora would never forget, and never name. Later, no aftershave, Pip said fiercely to Dora, shaking her head, just gin. First, after their mother died when Dora was fourteen, and then again, after what must have been a guilt-ridden hiatus for their father, when Merrill left for college. Pip was fifteen. His knowledge of their lives so intimate he knew when he didn't need to use a condom.

Merrill listened from the second bed, chilled; they were dredging up the past not to tell, but rather to remind her. They still thought it was only a matter of time till it all came back. Sighing deeply, Dora assured her that it took a lot to get through denial. And when she did, Pip said, they'd be here for her.

That night, Merrill probed her memory for the sounds, and tastes, and smells of her teenage years, the dark days after their mother's lingering death, when neighbors had turned their house into a commissary. Merrill cracked open her old bedroom door at the end of the hall, turned her head on her pillow toward the dim hall light, became fifteen again, and waited.

Her father never came to her.

Instead, she remembered how he clapped too loud at her clarinet recital—at all their recitals—how he'd insisted she do her homework before the dishes, how he'd called a neighbor to ask if all girls were wearing outlandish clothes like his daughters, and how he'd rolled his eyes and finally let them wear what they wanted. Later he had endured their poor choice of men, their engagements with alcohol and brief flirtations with drugs.

Next, Merrill tried to imagine the unimaginable. She listened from her bed, started him on the creaking path to her sisters' doorways. She watched him hesitate in shame, and curse his weak resolve, as he opened and closed each door. He lowered himself to his daughter, on his knees or stretched the length of each small form. He fumbled with Dora's flannel gown, or lowered his smooth, damp face to Pip, lifted her thin t-shirt. Had he ever said I'm sorry?

He hadn't come to Merrill then; he didn't come to Merrill now. How long before her sisters believed her? And what would she be left with?

The evening's drama hung over their next day at the hospital. Their father's form was even more insubstantial to Merrill, though his real weight still weighed, she knew, on her sisters' hearts. She watched him breathe. His hand in hers was hollow bone, transparent flesh. It was impossible to imagine this frail man, her father, pushing, panting. His strong shoulders, his muscled arms and taut neck would have drowned Merrill. How did Dora and Pip survive? When the doctor convened another family conference, they voted against extreme measures. Later, back at their hotel, Pip said the time for speaking up was running out.

"We don't know for sure he'll hear us," Dora said.

"The nurse said he would. If I have to get a megaphone, he'll hear us," Pip said.

The next morning, in a small conference room down the hallway from where their father's breathing was slowly ebbing away, Merrill said she had something she had to say. Dora first then Pip rose from their chairs to come to her.

"It's true," she said into the violent silence. "For all three of us." Her practiced gaze held steady, put to surprising use. She turned to Dora and said that she agreed with Pip, they needed to confront their father. "But separately. We have our own separate stories, our own separate lives." Dora took her hand, Pip her other hand and Merrill closed her eyes. She held on to her sisters' hands for dear life, and said, "I want to be last."

Together, they stood beside their father's bed, all on one side, as the nurse made an adjustment to the heart monitor on the other, called a doctor in to increase the dosage released by the morphine drip. Finally, touching each one of them lightly on the arm, she left them to their grief.

The shushing sounds of the intercom and clatter of mealtime trolleys filtered through the door behind them. Reaching high, Pip slid the white curtain on its track around the foot of their father's bed even though there was no one to hear what each was going to say. Their father's face was grayer than yesterday, his whiskered cheeks quivered beneath blue oxygen tubes.

Weeping, Dora shook her head at Pip and Merrill, saying "I can't do this," but Pip gave her a push and so she turned back to the white bed, his bony chest, his lean helpless arms. She bent down and said they were all here, once again. She took his hand in hers, held it for an instant then put it purposefully down. It would be the last time she would touch him. "Dad," she said. "There's something we need to say."

Pip tugged on Merrill's arm and they went out to wait in the hallway, beside the bright lights and dramatic monitoring systems of the ICU's nursing station. "She's whispering," Pip said. "But he'll hear her." Unaccountably, Merrill found herself wondering how elaborate Pip's cat hospital was. How did she arrange visiting hours for each pet? She pictured cat owners standing mute beside dull silver cages.

When Dora appeared, she held out her hand to Pip as if passing a baton in a relay, and Pip went in. Because she didn't want to hear Pip's voice, her words, Merrill followed Dora part way down the hall, rehearsing, rehearsing her own sister-role. Then a weeping Pip came out and with the same odd gesture, her hand finding Merrill's hand, she sent her in to have the final say.

She crossed the disinfected floor to stand by her father. Her father, still alive, but barely. Her father—still able to divide and conquer. Belatedly, she wished she knew what her sisters had said to him. Do accusations and forgiveness ever go together? She hoped she would someday know. And now his body was wringing out its last liquid on his brow.

As she smoothed the stiff white sheet across his shallow, shrunken chest, Merrill's heart thudded with astonishing betrayal and paralyzing love. "It's Merrill," she told him. "I came to say goodbye." Oh, how had her father and mother parted? The sisters had not been there for their final moment together. But she remembered her father's terrible grief after their mother's death, the enormous loss of her, and she could imagine his reluctance—more like loathing—to replace their mother with another woman, allow another woman's clothes to fill her closet, her strange scents and toiletries in their bathroom, her cookware in his wife's kitchen, her piano or books or paintings in his home, her voice chastising or complimenting or berating or praising his three daughters. Her ignorance of history. No, he'd have none of this; his only weakness was his need for what his two daughters could give—then.

And, selfishly, he'd needed one daughter to trust him, to receive his chaste and isolating love.

Merrill went to stand by her father. Surely this would kill him— his failing heart, her failing heart. She took his light right hand and made a fist of it, one pale bony finger at a time, and then in both of hers she held it to her heart.

"Why?" she said. "Why not me?"

She said it again. She whispered that he had left her alone once before, but she was not going to allow it a second time. She said she was going to pull back the curtain, she was going to walk out of this hospital room and join her sisters. Were his eyes wet? Had he heard her? Yes. She made one fist of their two fists and squeezed hard, and felt a return of pressure with his last and perfect strength. Then she opened his fingers one by one, placed his hand on the bed, and kissed his cheek, and then she turned away. Outside, Dora and Pip would be talking in low voices, their shoulders touching. But when she appeared they would part for her and, as they walked down the hallway, away from their father's dying, she would take her place between them.

Home Depot

"JAMES. JAMES, WHAT IS that big ugly orange building?" my father-in-law says, peering out the sliding door past our scruffy deck.

There is no hiding anything from Henry—especially anything that large. "Home Depot," I say.

My in-laws arrived after dark last night, and by then we'd closed the door to the deck and pulled shut the drapes. This is their first visit since they moved to Miami last winter. As usual, Henry was up at the crack of dawn. An hour ago, the coffee grinder pulverized the beans to powder. Dressed in a white golf sweater and ironed khakis, he's still staring at Home Depot. I'm in my ratty plaid bathrobe.

"It's so close to your house," he says. "Isn't this a residential neighborhood?"

I don't take the bait. I treat Henry's questions as if they are statements with which I have no argument. Wait till he sees the New and Used Gun Emporium, the three tattoo parlors, and all the fireworks stores that flank Home Depot. Seabrook is famously just over the Massachusetts state line. There's a long stretch of road leading into town where one side of the road is austerely Massachusetts and the other side a bustling, sleazy New Hampshire. No doubt Henry will want a tour today and will soon learn that we are just a mile from the Seabrook Nuclear Power Plant. Its unmistakable silhouette will surely lead to penetrating questions about the federal government's security measures and the town's evacuation procedures. Maybe my in-laws will leave early. But they are, after all, concerned parents. Ten years ago, in my mid-twenties, my parents died within a year of each other and I miss them: my father's sweet skepticism and my mother's discerning grace. I regret that Maida never met them. Maida who changed her name from Margaret in college, though her puzzled parents still call her Maggie. Maida who never changed her last name to mine. Not a complaint, I tell myself, merely an observation. I am surprised, however, that her parents still don't know the real reason we invited them to visit: Maida and I are embarking on a trial separation. One of us will be moving out.

Joining Henry on the deck, I give him the only good news. "Look closely down through the locust trees? There's a tiny creek—more like a marsh, actually a wetland—behind the house." I point with my coffee mug to the stand of trees hiding the low, fertile waters. "It separates us from Home Depot's parking lot." They often seem to build on wetlands—Seabrook and Medford, Mass.

Upstairs, the ladies are beginning to stir. Pipes are clanging and closet doors need oiling.

Henry is bending over the railing, his keen attention now focused on the marsh. "That's probably where all the mosquitoes are breeding. They feasted on us when we unpacked the car last night. Which reminds me that Pony said to ask if you have any Benadryl lotion."

Pony is a nickname I refuse to use when addressing my mother-in-law.

Henry elaborately scratches his arm, and I resist scratching my own three newly acquired bites. "The city sprays a couple times a year," I tell him.

He shakes his head. "More chemicals leaching into the water table. Well, maybe you can get the neighbors to sign a petition." Before they moved, Henry was an alderman in his tiny Indiana town, a town with no Home Depot within sixty miles. He was also the author of no fewer than twenty-three petitions.

"Maybe," I say. My own petition is pending with Maida, so I work harder to be a better son-in-law by asking, "A petition for—?"

"A tall fence. Get your neighbors to sign a petition asking Home Depot to put up a fence to hide their store. That way you won't have an orange landscape and what looks like a used-car lot in your backyard. And shady customers won't be thinking they might just wade across that buggy marsh and help themselves to a free computer or TV."

I snort into my mug—being one of Home Depot's best customers. I know the layout of the store so well I could work there: where the safety flashlights are shelved—not with flashlights; which floor surface will need a subfloor, something the literature only obliquely mentions; how to steer their heavy flat-bed carts up and down the aisles in a straight line.

"Those big chains are pretty open to local petitions," he says. "I could help you with the wording. The last petition I drew up was to block a detour that was going to cut into the nesting habitat of the wild turkey."

Evidently Henry has missed the serious pick-ups skulking in every driveway on our street; half are owned by contractors. We are the only people for blocks who drive a car. I feel guilty putting it off onto the neighbors, but I do it anyway, saying, "If the neighbors ever signed a petition it wouldn't be for a fence between us and Home Depot. Hell, their petition would be for a bridge."

"A bridge?" He turns and looks at me, light dawning on his flat face. I nod. It occurs to me that I could use his help, but I don't know how to ask. He sees me hesitate, then with a tightening of my robe, I am on my way upstairs to look for Pony's Benadryl and take a hot shower that I wish Maida would interrupt.

Too late. Her long hair is pulled into a tight knot I like to cup in the palm of my hand, before I set it loose to shadow her full breasts or brush my stomach. She's made our bed with military corners and is already dressed in jeans and a pullover.

"Your father's up," I tell her. When I tug on the zipper of her jeans she pulls my hand away. Reluctantly. Or maybe that is my imagination. She's still holding my hand, when a burst of loud static erupts, like a goose looking for its goslings or mate: *URRRKKKKKK*. Then: "Ernie to Building Four with the plane saw. Ernie to Building Four with the plane saw." Static again, *URRRRRRKKKKKKKKKKKKKKK*. Then silence. Downstairs, the glass slider lets out a squeal as Henry opens it and steps onto the deck.

Maida and I exchange the warmest glance we've shared in weeks.

I open our upstairs window to hear what Henry will hear. That ear-piercing *UURRRRRRKKKKK*.

Sure enough, he calls out as if I'm still listening to him no matter where I am in the house, "Do you two hear that all day?" His voice is so loud that Home Depot's Ernie-with-the-plane-saw also probably hears him.

Maida rolls her eyes. "I was hoping it would rain."

It is raining, a hard, hard rain, I want to say, but don't.

"Your turn to go down there. I've just been," I say to Maida. "Be sure to tell him that their PA system shuts down after four."

With a polite cough, Pony emerges from the guestroom where my computer is being held hostage. The walls still sport a border of gleeful carousels—it must have once been a nursery. Last spring, Maida put "strip the border" at the top of our to-do list, but I said to let it be, that it reminded me of my happy childhood, at which point she'd shrugged hugely, though she didn't ask if I was joking or serious. I actually don't know, myself. But the horses and lions still prance near the ceiling while I write software programs for a sedentary living.

Pony does not meet my gaze or notice my dismay that she is in full make-up and pearls, which means she has probably been up a while and heard our early morning argument. I wonder if she heard Maida's accusation that if we hadn't gotten married we might still be together. "So getting married was a bad thing," I asked her, though I knew she was referring to the terms of our engagement, terms I've been trying to rewrite. We agreed no kids three years ago when we set the wedding date. But now I wanted kids. More than one. Sons and daughters. Brothers and sisters. Siblings. Like my two sisters and brother. Their children my kids' cousins. An only child, Maida emphatically shakes her head at my talk of even one child. For the past year, I have felt a longing in my loins that is not sexual. It curls up around my heart and leaves me breathless, my arms aching to hold a child. At Home Depot I watch as fathers explain electricity or cement to a son or daughter. I watch kids tag along behind carts loaded with plans and lumber for swing sets, sand boxes, and elaborate tree houses. I smile and watch kids whine and cry, piss and spill gooey purple-colored liquids. It is called "Home" Depot, not "House," for a reason.

I want help from Henry and Pony, so I locate the Benadryl and present it to Pony as if it were a magic potion. "Good of Henry to remember," she says. It is true. Her right eye is swollen and red.

URRRRRRKKKKKKKK "Betty. Forklift to Trees and Shrubs. Betty: Forklift to Trees and Shrubs." URRRRRRRRRRRRRRKKKKKK. Maida probably likes the idea of Betty behind the wheel of the compact forklift, Betty in overalls, pressing the gas pedal with her steel-toed boots. I like the idea of Betty on the forklift too, steering a careful path through flooring, cabinetry, kitchen appliances to arrive at large flowering shrubs, but I also suspect Betty is underpaid with four kids at home helping to spend her paycheck. To give Maida credit, she probably imagines representing Betty pro bono in a lawsuit claiming wage discrimination, so her sympathy is certainly more useful than mine.

"What makes you think you'll be a good father?" Maida asked during this morning's argument. When I told her that wanting to be a good father would go a long way, she said, "Then go have your kids." An odd injunction, as if the rest of it was "And then come back." But we both know once gone I'm gone for good.

I shower in hot, hot water, and for the hundredth time berate myself for not knowing that children would one day matter to me. For not knowing that love could seep away from our marriage into a reservoir whose mysterious tides could not be reversed. URRRRRRKKKKKKKKK. I laugh because I can't tell if I'm crying. And then I dress for a Saturday of in-law entertainment.

Downstairs, Pony and Maida are cooking breakfast. I would offer to help but instead I admire their practiced moves. Maida is sautéing mushrooms for an omelette or quiche. I imagine Pony instructing a six-year old Maida in the culinary arts, and I picture her chubby fingers dipping into a bowl of pink icing. I try to picture Maida teaching our son or daughter how to mince garlic but—this is telling—I just can't.

Henry is standing in front of the fridge, perusing our magnetic photographs from British Columbia, Labrador, and Morocco. "Travel, not toddlers," Maida had chanted after the recent chaotic visit of my best friend, who'd had his second child in three years. Sleepless, we helped them repack their car with carriages, diaper pails, stuffed animals, snacks, and bottles. We'd just returned from Bella Coola and were already acquiring maps of Slovenia. "Travel, not toddlers," I repeated after her, but with a sharp pang I'd never felt before. There was no going back. My next daydreams were of a toddler strapped to my back, rounded arms around my neck, another, older toddler holding my hand as we navigated a particularly steep spot on our hiking trail. Maida following behind, identifying the calls of birds, carrying the newborn in a sling, beneath breasts alive with rich milk I'd tasted twice.

URRRRRRRRRRRRRRKKKKKKKKK. "Thibideaux to Outdoor Lighting. Thibideaux to Outdoor Lighting." *UUUUURRRRKKKKK.*

"That's Battle Harbor," I say to Henry who is peering at a photo of twin outhouses. I describe the tiny island off the coast of Labrador, where the indefatigable and noble Dr. Grenfell built one of the first hospitals. But Henry's gaze has moved past the photo to my list for Home Depot: screen for bathroom; caulking; half-inch washers.

"I see you're a regular customer," he said, a note of surprise in his voice.

Yeah, I think, I'd use the bridge.

After breakfast I suggest to Henry that a trip to Home Depot might be a good way to pass an hour. He is game, but Maida objects. "Dad doesn't want to follow you around while you moon over BBQ grills and lawn chairs." Pony waves her hand as if we've left already, assuring me she will go another time. You might not have another opportunity, I want to say, but we still haven't broken our news.

Henry insists on driving. We turn right out of our drive and go to the end of the long street, away from the disconcerting view of Home Depot. There he turns right to the light, passes a tattoo parlor, the fireworks stores, a vacuum cleaner repair shop, then takes another right which leads us to Home Depot's expansive parking lot. I point out it is the long way around. As usual, the parking lot is alive with cars and pickups and the static voice instructing employees where they and their forklifts or plane saws are needed next.

We are greeted at the door by a man Henry's age wearing the familiar orange vest. His name tag says "Fred" and his greeting is so warm that if he wasn't decked out in the store's uniform, my father-in-law might have thought they knew each other. Even so, he shakes the man's hand and assures him we are happy to be here.

Afterwards Henry mutters, "I wonder what hardware store he used to own. How can he be so happy?"

I snag a shopping cart and Henry shuffles after me, impressed, I can tell, by how well I know my way around the aisles of wheelbarrows and power tools, through nuts and bolts to a wall of washers.

While I am hunting for the right size and thickness, Henry says he thinks he'll wander around some on his own. "I didn't know they had a gardening section," he says. "Thought it was all construction stuff."

I tell him my list won't take long and I'll look for him there. Today, with Henry accompanying me, I easily resist the temptation to buy a leather tool belt, which anyway would always look too new around my waist. Every once in a while, a contractor comes in with his still on: supple, broken in, stained a golden sienna from sweat and grime. I envy that weight as if it were another set of balls, capable of anything. They sell a miniature tool belt for kids, with almost as many loops and rivets as the grownup belt. I will treat my girls the same as I treat my boys and vice versa. But I can't imagine who their mother will be; I am still in love with Maida, but I suspect that love can be replaced by longing. I think she is not in love with the me that wants children.

Today, a harassed-looking father is hauling his wailing kid down from a red rolling ladder. The father clearly smells the poopy diaper. I note that the kid has the father's big ears, and my left hand involuntarily goes to my own left ear, which sticks out further than the right. Maida used to say "the more handles the better."

I find the right size washer, then hunt for Henry. He is not in gardening, and I imagine he is standing impatiently near the car, peering past the roofs of too many pickups, trying to identify our house through the trees. He is probably hoping he can't see it, but he will be disappointed. Undaunted, perhaps energized, he will move on to plotting where the fence should go, drafting the first lines of the petition, for which he will expect me to gather signatures by going door to door.

He's not at the car. Now my hope is that he hasn't decided the marsh can't be all that soggy or deep and, adventurer that he is, hasn't tried to wade back to my house. I can't remember if he is wearing his golfing shoes, or if golfing shoes have cleats.

I return to garden supplies, though I fear failure. But there Henry is, lounging at the checkout counter tucking a silver credit card into his wallet.

"You're not going to believe this," he says, and he's right. He tells me that Pony has always wanted an outdoor fountain, but nothing cutesy like a fish spouting water, or a cupid pouring water from a chubby jug, and absolutely nothing that gurgles. He says he has found the perfect fountain. "Japanese design, a surprise for Pony. The neighbor's grandkids will love it." He says it will be delivered the week they're back.

He is right; the fountain is beautiful. Oblong granite stones interwoven in two towers three feet high, water cascading from one stone to another. Elegant even. Mesmerizing. A girl about six or seven, in frazzled pigtails, is holding her hand very still in the waterfall. She doesn't notice us. Henry points to her shoes, which are soaked, and we both smile. I love him for his enthusiasm and Pony for her taste. He is happy. On our way out, he wants to know if I think his daughter would want an identical fountain. I tell him, "I'll bring her by and let you know. Or maybe you should ask her."

Pony and Maida have rearranged the living room—something I've wanted Maida to do with me for months. The couch and two chairs now allow more intimate conversation. Pony is polishing an end table and Maida is moving a lamp nearer the couch. "Perfect," Pony says, and looks to me for approval. I tell her she's read my mind, as if I am the son she knows only too well. Suddenly I am surprised to be missing them already. Maybe Henry and Pony should adopt me, or I them. A wave of grief washes me onto the couch where I sink with the knowledge that they are not going to be the grandparents of my children. The cushions feel like quicksand. No one notices because Henry is extolling the virtues of Home Depot to his disbelieving daughter, his attentive wife.

His secret purchase gives lunch a festive air that cannot be dispelled by our own looming secret. As we open the second bottle of Pinot Grigio, it occurs to me that Maida's parents might be expecting the opposite of what we have to say because they talk of friends' grandchildren, family reunions. Maida must sense this—she hurriedly begins to gather up our empty plates.

As she serves a peach pie Pony made an hour ago, she says, "James and I have something to tell you."

"Oh, we thought so," Pony says, and rises to give Maida a hug, her pearls swinging against Maida's long hair.

Maida catches her hand, ducks her head to loosen the pearls from her hair. "It isn't what you think," she says.

Henry and Pony's eyes widen, parents' frightened eyes; they look to Maida then to me, and finally to each other for comfort. I wonder why Maida thought we needed a visit for this news, a couples' visit.

"James and I—we're separating," Maida says.

"Oh, Maggie, dear," Pony says, and Henry's bewildered gaze seeks mine. Our bond over Home Depot is stretching, stretching.

"I'm moving out," Maida says. And here she looks at me. She knows that "moving out" is new, and I thought still undecided.

Henry says "Please don't do anything too hasty," and Pony's "are you sure you want to do this" isn't a question, but rather her clear and tearful dismay.

I refuse to break down. I push back my chair and stand up, announcing that I'm going to put the lawn mower to work. "Henry, Pony." I duck my head at them, sad, because they belong to Maida. "You all will want to talk."

And what will Maida say? James has decided he wants to have children, and I do not. Or you knew I never wanted to have children. It is true that Maida said this all through law school and our courtship.

Her parents probably never believed her. And I didn't know my own desires. I cry as I put my shoulders to the task of pushing the mower around our green puddle of a lawn, wanting kids trailing after me, squabbling over the rake, throwing fresh grass high into the summer air.

Has she already found an apartment? I think I suspected this. Over the roar of my lawnmower, the music begins again: *URRRRRRRKKKKKKKKK.* It will be me here, starting a new life. Falling out of love, hoping to recover from a broken heart and waiting for the bridge to Home Depot. As I take a wide arc, the orange building comes into view, and I recall the ride home with Henry, who was still aglow with his purchase of the fountain for Pony and the neighbors' grandkids. Maybe he was planning how he would take Maida aside and ask if she wanted one too, seeing his own grandchildren gleeful over the twin fountains—one here and one in Florida. He pulled out of the Home Depot lot onto the bustling highway, and as he took the first, then the second, then the third left turn of the trip onto our long street, he said, "You're right. It is the long way round."

Breathe

For L.S.

BEGINNING WITH THE VERY first fire at the unused Rotary Hall and the police report of suspected arson, Paul was fascinated. He secretly collected every newspaper clipping he could find. As each story hit the evening news, he took in the wailing sirens of two a.m. alarms, the purple lakes of smoke hovering above town, the surprising choice of scene: an old harness factory, the boarded-up house on Third and Main where drugs changed hands like candy.

His mom would come in from peeling or slicing in the kitchen, and his dad would be kicked back in his recliner, one eye on the sports page, while tiny cobalt flames from the night before raged and died on the TV screen.

"What's this world coming to?" Paul's mom said more than once, a knife or potato peeler suspended in the air. She worked the ER at Community Hospital four days a week, taught biology at nurse's training, and Paul guessed she knew exactly what the world was coming to.

"They'll find him sooner or later," his Dad would say. Then he'd tell Paul to get the new glove from his ninth birthday and they'd head out to the street so Paul could practice his pitch. He was always surprised at the pinpoints of light, the heat in his father's eyes. "You gotta try and make the team, and that requires lots of practice," his father said their last time out.

Paul was tempted to tell his father about a mean kid named

Jeremy, who practiced his throwing arm on birds and flowers and occasionally on Paul or Billy Fraily. It used to be Jeremy started all the fights, but now Paul started a few on his own. He could tell when Jeremy was working up to a fight and all Paul had to do was point at the purple birthmark covering Jeremy's entire left cheek. "Your kids are going to have bigger birthmarks than that. It's in your genes," Paul told him, adding that sometimes it looked like a badge but more often like rotten grapes. Right now Jeremy was first team pitcher.

"What if I don't make the team?" Paul asked as his father placed Paul's fingers on the ball for a breakaway pitch. His father's eyes had narrowed.

"You're my son. You got to learn survival."

His father was big on survival. It had to do with Vietnam and his trouble sleeping, and why he kept saying no when Paul asked about getting a dog. "Come on, Frank," his mother said last week. "Every boy needs a dog. You're worse than when you came back." His father had shrugged and said he'd learned to sleep light over there because too many guys were on drugs. "When those guys sat on watch I was on watch with 'em. Couldn't trust 'em." He said he'd get on the radio to them at odd times to keep their ears in practice. He said it might be years before he'd sleep OK. Till then, he didn't need anything moving around at night, or any damn dog triggering his nightmares. The slightest noise and he'd be reaching for his gun, so he didn't want guns in the house either. He'd said it again to Paul yesterday: "No dog. They eat dogs over there."

"Frank!" his mother said.

"No dog."

Every time a fire was reported on the evening news, Paul dreamed about it the following night. He didn't think of these dreams as nightmares. His news clippings came from Mr. Felco, their next door neighbor, because Paul's father said he didn't want any world news coming into the house—especially bad news about what the US military was or wasn't doing. Mr. Felco sat in his wheelchair all day filling out racing forms and watching reruns of movies and soaps. Mr. Felco's wife had died the previous year, so Paul ran errands for him after school, took out garbage, washed dishes, and stacked his day-old newspapers on the back porch, where he'd tuck the front page into his jacket. Headlines grew larger when the police and fire department figured out the fires were no freak of nature. *Arson* is a short word, so they used it often, far more than *incendiary* or *conflagration* or *pyromaniac*. *Firebug* was Mr. Felco's word. Paul snuck his mother's pinking shears to cut out the columns of stories and photographs. Then he rolled back the faded rug beside his bed and threw out the collection of dog pictures he'd cut from magazines. They didn't look much like dogs anyway: too sleek or fluffy, or deeply wrinkled or with ankles as thin as a garden hose, more like exotic animals, not pets. Dogs that wouldn't know what to do with a stick or a ball. He wanted a dog-dog. He lined up his new clippings in rows under the rug's edge. At night, when he walked back and forth, they crackled like dry leaves catching fire. Sometimes, he could feel their heat through his socks.

Paul was at school when the police came.

His father had gotten off work and was probably starting a second beer while brewing pots of Theraflu for Paul's mother, who was home sick. Her eyes were red when she told Paul. She said she didn't even get to change out of her bathrobe or tell his father goodbye—they came and went that fast. Too fast, Paul hoped, to find his stash of clippings. "You wait," she said, "Where do they get off—blaming him for those fires. They'll find out they've got the wrong guy."

"When?" Paul said.

"Don't worry," his mother said, hands on his shoulders in a gesture his father often used. "Soon. He'll be home soon. I bet in time to see you pitch your first game of the season."

"No way," Paul said, thinking, What first game? Especially with Jeremy still practicing on birds. He wanted his father home, but how can you fear and want the exact same thing?

"Now go do your homework. Aren't you writing that report on

genes?" She gave him a little push, saying maybe coach would fill in with extra practice time. After seeing him off, she got back on the phone, her voice shaky, talking bail and bonds.

Paul locked his door, took off his shoes, and walked back and forth on the border of his rug.

Then, lifting the frayed top edge, he slid out the first account from nine months before—the old harness factory on faded, yellow newsprint, itchy with rug hairs. He placed his father at the scene of each fire, reconnoitering the territory like he'd do for his job at the gas company, measuring streets for gas mains and repairing faulty pipes. Maybe arson was in their genes? Like his father's red hair and sharp green eyes, his long big toe. His mother had blonde hair, and a million freckles mostly on the left side of her face, but as far as Paul could tell she hadn't shown up in him yet.

He knew this for sure: his father would hate jail. It would be too much like the army—counting heads, sitting around, waiting for something to happen and dreading it at the same time. His father said that of all the things you learned to kill in the army, what you wanted most to kill was time—something he hoped Paul never had to learn.

He pictured his father lying on his back on some narrow cot, hands folded behind his head, eyes closed. Maybe he'd be thinking about their pitching practice, or better yet, their fishing trips when he taught Paul how to breathe underwater, how to wade the creeks without making a sound or causing a ripple larger than a trout catching flies. "Called survival. At times, we hid in those putrid rivers so long you could feel yourself rotting from the toes up. But at least it meant you were still alive." After one really bad nightmare his father woke screaming, and while Paul shivered in the hallway, his father had described to Paul's mother the stretchers full of arms and legs they collected after devastating firefights. Bodies half-burned, parts strewn everywhere and how the guys tried to put them back together. Someone filling a body bag would call out "I need an arm" and someone else would yell "black or white," and depending on the reply, "Can't help you there" or "I got two—right or left?" But even Paul knew two legs or two arms didn't mean they got the person put back together right. If the genes were wrong maybe the body parts would fight it out. An arm could get rejected or rot.

A week later, Paul asked his father what a body bag looked like. He said that he'd watched *War and Pieces* with Mr. Felco but they didn't seem to use body bags in that war. In that war bodies were carted away or just left to the weather.

"'Peace' not 'pieces,'" his mother said. "*War and P-E-A-C-E.*"

His father sat there at the dinner table, not answering, his head in his hands. Paul's mother moved to knead his father's shoulders, saying that he should talk to someone. And to Paul she said "You have to stop listening so hard." Why, he'd wondered, when listening hard had kept his father alive.

He put his clippings away and smoothed down the rug, leaving room for news of his father's arrest. Bottom line, he wanted his father home. Even if it meant his father would be complaining about nightmares, or keeping tabs on all the walks Paul gave up to the other team, or saying no to a dog. Paul wanted him home because he had questions he needed to ask.

His father never did get out on bail even though his case didn't come up till two months later. In all that time, his mother refused to let Paul visit. "County jail's no place for kids. Write him letters," she said. She brought home letters his father had written to him asking for reports on school and stuff, and sure Paul wrote back, but he knew a letter wasn't the way to tell him about their secret collection of clippings.

When school let out for the summer, the third side of Paul's rug was almost full with news of his father's arrest and upcoming trial. Paul didn't walk on that side. Headlines had gotten smaller again and soon the articles were buried on the inside pages with ads for ladies underwear, recipes and world news. Mr. Felco had gotten more interested in the papers so Paul had to wait a few days before he could bring them home. This week he'd begun a collection of matches and was up to six books, mostly from Arlene, his mother's friend from work, who came over after shift to talk and plot while she moved from room to room, still in her white uniform, leaving nail files, half-smoked cigarettes and matches in her wake—matches from Rita's Place, The Bombshelter, Sweet Licks.

Because his mother wouldn't let Paul go to court for the trial, he had to catch it on nightly news. Each day after school he went next door to old Mr. Felco, who said, "Yo, Paul," when Paul walked in. He'd learned "yo" from TV. Paul did his homework at the dining room table while Mr. Felco zapped the tube and said what he always said: "The people who write these soaps understand the true state of the world, more than those bozos down in Washington." Today he added, "Those generals weren't too good to boys like your dad." And then he hit the remote.

As music for *Heaven's Bounty* soared into the room, he said, "*Heaven's Bounty* did arson ten years ago." Paul said that was before he was born. Mr. Felco said too bad he missed it 'cause he didn't think they'd sold out yet to reruns.

An hour later, Paul joined Mr. Felco for *Cradle to Grave* till his mother called him through Mr. Felco's screen door. Her eyes glistened and her nose was rawly red. It was plain his father had been convicted. Mr. Felco didn't ask any questions, just told her to send Paul over anytime.

Walking home, his mother squeezed Paul's face into the belt of her coat. "Don't you believe it," she said. Her chest heaved above his head like a storm and he thought, but what about all their clippings.

Arlene was bustling around. She put glasses in the freezer and mixed up a pitcher of margaritas while his mother went up to the bedroom to call his grandfather who was in the Veteran's home with Alzheimer's. She said she better prepare him for hearing his name on TV since Paul's father was a "Junior."

Paul was asking Arlene about her dog—a golden retriever not good at retrieving—when his mother returned. Slumping into a chair, she reported that her father-in-law said he was leaving the Vets home and going right out to enlist tomorrow. "He's forgotten every awful war experience he ever had. Jesus, but look what it took." When Paul asked how soon he could see his father, she said as soon as he got to where they were sending him and visiting hours were set.

All evening, a parade of neighbors came and went like they did when old Mrs. Felco died, except no one seemed to know what to say with his father not here, but still alive. Two people brought casseroles. No one sent flowers.

A week later, the judge handed down his father's sentence. On the way home from Mr. Felco's, his mother explained how the judge took into account all the fires the army had encouraged his father to set in Vietnam, and how the US had used napalm to burn the country bare. Arlene was making Bloody Marys. Her earrings sparkled on the table. She and Paul's mother were still in their court clothes—white blouses, skirts, high heels.

"Paulie," Arlene said, ruffling his hair, "It's been a hard day. Now you go watch TV and let your mom and me talk."

As Paul listened from the next room, his mother told Arlene how his father had learned to do terrible things in the war. Paul could tell she was crying as she said he'd talked about it more in the past month than he ever had before. It was all coming out. How six radio operators had died in his arms. When his operators died, he held their guts together and felt their lives drain away. All that blood. Eventually he wouldn't let himself get close to any of them. He'd learn only their last names and would tell them "stay two steps behind me, one on my right and one on my left." A new recruit the guys named Firebird insisted on reading his letters to Paul's father. He'd say, "But you got to hear this, Daddy Rabbit" when Paul's father refused to listen, and in the end he said they always got through to him. "The worst," he'd told her, "was sending out two men on reconnaissance. There'd be no eye contact. Everyone knew they were going to die." How to choose was a terrible decision, he'd said. Every two months, his CO would put him down for R & R but afterwards they kept sending him back in. He finally started turning down the medals. He couldn't cry anymore. "He never put any of this in letters," she said. "It's all been inside." She stopped talking and the kitchen was silent except for the sound of ice cubes sliding back and forth in glasses. Over Arlene's murmur, she continued. She said the first month he'd been home they'd watched a TV movie about a street gang and, he'd nodded calmly at the screen and said, "They look like they'd be hard to kill."

"Oh sweetie," Arlene said.

"I don't want to be a nurse at home, too," his mother whispered. Paul had to strain to hear her say, "And Paul will never have a sister at this rate. Some guys from his company who stop by every year or so never had any kids. Couldn't. Things happened over there we'll never know."

"Lucky your house is paid off," Arlene said,

"Could we not jump to the bright side yet?" his mother flared.

Paul had to ask, had to know. He carried a pillow in front of him, pressed against his heart. "Did the judge say anything about genes?"

"Dammit, Paulie. You were listening again," his mother said, wiping her eyes with a dish towel. "So you know we weren't talking genes. Where do you get genes?"

"But you said my red hair came from Dad, that genes got passed down."

"Paulie," Arlene said. "Don't think about—"

"He just does. He thinks. He's that kind of kid. So wait," his mother said, holding up her flattened hand to Arlene. Then she pulled the pillow from Paul's arms and sent it flying. She put his face between her cold hands. "War isn't in your genes. Sending men to die isn't in your genes," she said, with a fierceness Paul found terrifying.

Arlene put her hand on his mother's arm and shook it. "Please stop, stop that talk." She pushed his mother into a chair and put the pillow on her lap. To Paul, she said, "I'll bet you're hungry. I am even if you aren't." She handed Paul an empty cereal box to throw away and set to washing the morning's dishes with a great clatter. Water whooshed into the sink; knives and forks collided. Steam rose. "I brought a casserole," she said. "Heat it up."

Their gas stove was ancient and had to be lit with a match. Paul watched as his mother struck a match, efficiently, purposefully, but then she stood there transfixed by the tiny flame.

Hands dripping water, Arlene backed up three steps and blew it out. "Frank probably used a lighter," she said.

"And kerosene," Paul said. "In the army they used napalm, but I don't think he could get it here."

When both women swung around to look at him hard, he backed out of the kitchen, saying it was almost time for the news.

His father was the big story on local TV. "Frank Cronin, who a week ago was found guilty on five counts of arson, was sentenced today," the anchor said. They showed his father being led away in handcuffs. His head was down and his suit jacket flapping. Paul bet his pockets didn't have any matches in them. On TV, Paul's mother and Arlene bobbed behind him. His mother had her hand out as if to keep him steady and Arlene was wearing sunglasses though anyone could tell it was about to rain.

"Oh, Paul, you shouldn't have to be seeing this," his mother said, her voice catching, as she patted the cushion beside her on the couch. Paul settled into her arms, his eyes on the screen.

Next, they showed before and after pictures of the abandoned Rotary hall, the druggie house, and the harness factory as they told about the suspicious nature of the fires, the witness who had spotted his father's pickup, his fingerprints on the can of kerosene. The pictures of the harness factory were old. Black and white. Drifts of snow covered the bottoms of the windows. One picture inside the factory showed boys Paul's age wearing flat caps and short pants like Babe Ruth's baseball uniform.

"Why aren't they in school?" Paul asked. His mother was big on school.

"Look at their clothes, Paul. The short pants, long heavy socks. Horses pulling the wagon. That picture was taken at least a hundred years ago," his mother said. "Those poor kids. It was way before child labor laws." Her voice was almost normal—like when she was helping with his school reports on bacteria or the human eye or talking about work—so he knew she'd be OK.

•

At the playing field, Jeremy called, "Hey, Paulie, your pitching's getting worse." He was throwing a hard ball at his captive catcher, Billy Frailly. "I hear your dad won't be home for a while."

Paul could have told him that.

"And there ain't been a fire since he got arrested. My dad said 'what more proof do they need?'" Wheeling, Jeremy blazed a hard fast ball at Paul, who stopped it with the heel of his gloveless hand. Billy Fraily snickered.

Paul didn't throw the ball back to Jeremy; he walked it over to him, his hand numb with pain, and slammed the ball into his glove. Aiming well, he poked Jeremy's cheek hard with his index finger.

"That's not a birthmark," Paul told him. "That's a deathmark."

That evening, when Jeremy's mother called Paul's mother to complain about Jeremy's torn shirt and bloody nose, Paul figured it was time to act.

The next day, he strapped on his father's old army belt and pack, his tin canteen, and rode his bike up and down the streets. Wavering heat mirages rose from the pavement as Paul scouted the town for what his father saw. He pictured him on his lunch break, wolfing down a sandwich before going out on reconnaissance, like he did in Nam. He'd feel the grime of black lines smudged under his eyes, the damp rustle of leaves from trees whose names he didn't know taped to his helmet, or woven into a net, his feet deep in muck. His father would remember as if it were only yesterday. He'd drive slow and deliberate, squinting the town's blocks into long terraced stretches of rice paddies capable of hiding whole hordes of tiny submerged Viet Cong. He'd be looking for sagging huts—"They were that country's landmines, those deserted villages," his father once said. The matches in Paul's pocket felt puny for the job they had to do, the man they had to save. He imagined headlines—once more in big type: ARSON AGAIN. Then in smaller type: Convicted Arsonist in Jail. What would Jeremy's father and the police make of that?

His search ended beyond the high school football field, at the town cemetery. Bordered by a low stone wall, the cemetery hadn't been mowed the whole summer because the town voted down new taxes. Wild grass grew high and yellow like the jungle his father described burning, burning after the tremendous silence from fire raids and their momentary vacuum of air. His father said in Nam the sun's heat was so fierce that even the insects flew at half speed. He said there were twenty-seven species of poisonous snakes they forgot to mention at Fort Bragg. He said that sometimes Vietnam was deathly beautiful.

Paul propped his bike against a broken wooden gate and waded in through the tall grass and weeds till he found a flat tombstone just right for laying out his supplies. Knife. Matches. He'd have to leave fast. Carved words read:

Elmer Wissle, 1894—1918
Husband and Father
And His Country's Fallen Son.

Wissle's gravestone was flaking at the corners and covered with scraggly brush, not getting the care it deserved. Eight tall trees flanking the sides of the graveyard would give his fire height. He hoped his father would be able to watch it on the news. He hoped his father would notice all the lessons he'd given Paul about survival.

Paul used his father's army knife to cut and rake together a pile of dry grass, then reached wider to gather twigs from recent thunderstorms. The matchbook was from Sousa's Bar and Grill. He would not Close Before Striking. He felt dizzy from bending over but when he looked up the sun's glare forced his eyes back down, and its afterimage became a ball of fire as he struck a single match. The flame wavered and descended almost to his fingers before he blew it out. It didn't smell like anything his father described. The sun's image faded to a tiny dot, so this time he put two matches together for a stronger flare. Holding his breath, he lowered his cupped hands toward the heap of twigs. Flame to fire. His eyes were wet with sweat and longing. What did it take for someone to start a fire? What did it take for his father to start a fire? To go to war?

He blew the matches out.

He couldn't do it, not even to help his father survive. Why? Was it because he wasn't being tracked and hunted to ground, to riverbed, or being haunted in his sleep? Or maybe there was no one and nothing out there he'd learned to hate enough to kill.

He swept his supplies into his father's backpack. The water in the canteen was warm. He drank it all. Suddenly, the heat of the afternoon contained a sound he'd know anywhere. It was the rattle of his father's pickup, the clanking of the tailpipe his father gleefully tolerated, saying that after Nam it was pure luxury to let people know he was coming.

His mother was still in her nurse's uniform. Her face gleamed with sweat and her long hair was ratty from the wind. After slamming the door, she walked over to his bike then looked around, calling his name.

He shouldered his father's backpack and went out to meet her.

As he lifted his bike into the back of the pickup, she said she'd been hunting for him for over an hour, that Mr. Felco was beside himself trying to comfort her with stories of foiled kidnappings from his soaps. Arlene had talked her into scouting before calling the police. "It's lucky I spied your bike. What on earth were you doing in there?"

What could he say? He tucked his father's backpack near the bike and brought the canteen with him into the truck.

"You're feeling pretty bad about all this, aren't you Paulie?"

He had to say something—anything—or he would cry. "I want a baby brother," he said. "Or a dog."

"A dog," she said. "You know your father—"

"I want a dog." He didn't back down.

"The dog I could do," she told Arlene later when they'd come home from the Animal Rescue League. All three of them had gone to the store for dog food and a dog bed Arlene predicted the puppy would never use. Paul stuck it in the closet and settled the puppy on his second pillow. The dog was brown with big ears and a skinny tail. It would probably never get its picture in a magazine. "I'll tell your father we have a dog," she said. "The time has come."

Things settled down. Soon, instead of Paul's father, people in town were talking about the missing councilman presumed to be accompanied by the missing twenty thousand dollars from the county building's safe. Three weeks later, his mother put on pink lipstick and drove them to the state penitentiary two hours away. It was a minimum-security prison which meant Paul's father could walk around with them when they got there. "Visitors," his mother said into a microphone as if they were ordering fast food take-out. Low gray buildings were strung together with gray airless breezeways. All the rooms were painted gray or green and dimly lit.

His father's hair was very short and not as red. He was thinner. Paul and his mother stepped into hugs they couldn't seem to leave. They all must have planned not to cry.

"Tour, who wants a tour?" his father said. His room was small and neat, with a photograph of Paul and his mother that used to be on the mantle, now on a shelf with books on narrow gauge railroads, famous rivers of the world.

When Paul's mother said she had packages in the car that she needed to clear through the front office, his father suggested he and Paul take the tour first. Paul knew she was giving them time alone.

A guard unlocked an iron door to the courtyard. Paul's father nodded to another man in similar clothes who was being pulled toward a cement bench by a young girl in a bright yellow dress. As they walked around the grounds, his father put his hands on Paul's shoulders and steered him like a train. Saving his questions for later, Paul told him about not making the A team in little league and about the new dog. He said it was still in the puppy stage and that his mother said there must be a word for training dogs. It wasn't toilet training she said.

"House training," his father said. "We'll tell her when she comes back." He said to let Mr. Felco know he hadn't missed one episode of *Cradle to Grave* since he'd been in prison.

Paul repeated what Mr. Felco said the afternoon his father was convicted: that *Heaven's Bounty* did arson ten years ago.

His father stopped steering Paul and they coasted to a stop. "Haven't given up on your old man, have you?"

Paul squinted up at his father then looked around to see if anyone could hear. "What were you going to burn down next?" It took his breath away to say it.

His father hesitated, looking Paul in the eye—his green eyes to Paul's green eyes. "Hey Paul. What is this? Research time?"

"I bet I can guess," Paul said.

"It wasn't like I had a mission," his father said. "Or any plan like the Big Brass claimed they had for Nam, but sure as shit didn't."

"The cemetery," Paul said. He studied his father's face.

His father threw Paul an imaginary pitch. "No, not the cemetery." He said he had too much respect for the dead. And when he got out of this place, he said he was going to take a trip with other veterans, guys like himself, go back to Nam, visit one or two of their cemeteries, look up some of the soldiers they'd been fighting against. Like a pilgrimage. Maybe take Paul and his mother when Paul was older. When he set to steering Paul again, Paul's shoulders felt lower and weak with relief. His father talked while he steered. "It was like the war, Paulie. Sooner or later, it had to end."

Paul took photographs of the puppy to show his father. "Now that's a dog," his father said. Kids in the neighborhood came by to teach the dog to play fetch. Jeremy watched from the sidewalk, the front wheel of his bike nudging the edge of their lawn, his birthmark flaming with puzzled heat.

The dog still wasn't house-trained—"your father said that was the word we were looking for," his mother told him—and Paul's rug was evidence enough. The clippings grew yellow and damp. His room smelled. He stopped walking around in his socks.

A week later, the dog barked. Standing in front of the door, it barked again. A sharp, urgent bark. "About time," his mother said, watching from the doorway as the dog lowered his flat backend into a squat, ran a few steps in the grass, then raised his leg to the oak tree.

It happened a second time, same day. "Home free," his mother said. "It's probably safe to send your rug out for a good cleaning."

Paul threw away the clippings. It felt like he'd put out a fire and was coming up for air.

On their last fishing trip, before the harness factory fire, Paul and his father had been up to their knees in a narrow creek, forlornly casting silver loops of fishing line, swatting flies. The day's heat was keeping the trout deep and sluggish. Giving up on fish—but only on fish, Paul realized now—his father had waded over to the bank and broken off a tall, hard reed. He blew air through it, tickling Paul's neck, to show Paul that it was hollow inside.

"You can hide under water for hours with one of these," he said. "We could hear them on the banks looking for us and we'd be hunkered down, five, six men, with our reeds only an inch above the water."

His father broke off a second reed and squatted low in the warm, lazy current. He held out his hand to Paul, who crouched down beside him, buoyant in the shallow water. Then he put the reed to Paul's lips and said, "Lean your head back and let yourself sink under, slowly, slowly. Don't make a sound. Now breathe. Breathe in and out through the reed. Breathe." And Paul did.

Invention Needs Design

HIS COFFEE BREAK OVER, Luke was passing the bank of phones on the sidewalk in front of the lot when one of them rang. He picked it up, said hello, and immediately a distraught woman's voice pleaded with him to look for her lost pair of gloves, deep blue stretch velvet with silver sequins at the wrist. "Don't see them anywhere," he said. "How far down the street do you want me to walk?" He could see Darrin sitting on his stool in the parking booth thirty yards away, alert, watching him. "Street? What street?" she said. "Isn't this The Downtown Cafe?" When Luke said no, that she was talking to a pay phone on the street, she said "my ass," and hung up. "My ass," Luke repeated—a good story to tell Darrin.

Since his sister June's death the previous spring, Luke had been wondering what he'd ever want to do again. This semester he'd hit bottom and after drafting class a week ago, he told Darrin that it was either dropping out of design school or finding a job. Darrin protested, "Man, you can't leave me. What about the company I designed for us?" Darrin was black and so thin that unless his clothes touched bone, they hung straight down like a plumb line. "Anyway, I have just the thing for you," Darrin said, and went on to describe the job at Kenmore, parking cars for big tips. Good amount of down time. "Guy quit just yesterday. I'll tell Vince I know someone who needs a job."

Two nights later, Vince was giving Luke the tour. The lot was on the edge of Kenmore Square, snug next to a low building, a nice piece of real estate, close to the clubs, Fenway Park. On the left, almost to the corner, newspaper stands lined the sidewalk across from the bank of pay phones. The subway roared out of its cave down Commonwealth Avenue and kept on going to more schools and colleges and Boston's pricey suburbs.

"Cars pull up to this here gate and you push the button to let them in," Vince said. He pushed a red button and the grubby, white arm of the gate rose; another push and it sank into place with a clang. "Then you take their money. If it ain't full or busy they park themselves. When it's busy they pull up, leave the keys and you shoehorn the car in wherever it will go. Tag the key and hang it on this board. Nothing to it." Vince waved his arm at the gates, the twenty plus cars dotted around the lot, tagged keys, and Darrin, whose bored, skinny frame was leaning against the cramped booth's door. "Darrin here can fill you in. It's a two-man job even though nights ain't busy, except for Red Sox games. Daytime's busiest. I've seen grown women cry when we turned them away." Vince winked at Darrin. "That's what you want, Darrin. Women crying for you." Luke thought not, but he laughed to get the job. "No drugs or booze or your ass is grass." Vince dinged the cash register, extracted all the twenties, left three, and sent Darrin to bring his car around.

"Vince is no trouble," Darrin said as he lowered the gate behind Vince's silver Porsche. "He knows I study on the job. Thinks he's putting me through art school. And if he ever needs a crack criminal lawyer I'll surprise him with my father's business card."

Tonight, with time crawling by, Luke told Darrin about the call from the pissy woman looking for her sequined gloves and, as usual, it gave Darrin an idea—everything did. "Where's that sweater someone dropped in the lot yesterday?" Darrin poked through telephone books and boxes till he found it. "Wait here," he told Luke, and headed out to the sidewalk. He draped the sweater over the fence behind the phone bank, jotted down the numbers of two phones, and returned, saying, "Watch and see what happens."

Several people passed briskly by, then a noisy group of students. Darrin didn't make a move till a woman in a shiny orange raincoat came strolling down the street on the end of a black terrier's leash. Then he dialed the number.

From the booth Luke could hear a faint, mournful ring.

Puzzled, the woman in the orange raincoat stopped and looked around, then moved toward the phone, dragging the terrier after her. When she answered, Darrin went into a spiel about using that same phone just hours ago and hanging his sweater over the fence while he made a call. "Do you see a sweater anywhere nearby?" he asked, then explained it was a special gift from his deaf mother in Tennessee who was coming to visit next month and expected him to be wearing it when he met her at the Greyhound station.

The woman peered at the sweater and finally asked, "What color?" and Darrin said, "Gray. Slate gray."

"Well, yes, I do see a gray sweater," the woman said tentatively and Darrin cut in with great, that's great, now the problem was getting the sweater back; he couldn't take a chance on her leaving it there for someone else to find. She was mute, but they could see her shaking her head.

Then Darrin said, "Hey, I got an idea. See the parking lot on the corner? Just up from the phones?" Soon she was peering at their booth where Darrin had his hand cupped around the mouthpiece. "Should be a guy working the booth? Sometimes two. Nice guys. I park in that lot all the time." Luke shook his head as Darrin instructed her to leave it with the guys at the booth, explain the situation to them. Say he'd be over tomorrow evening to pick it up.

She looked at the phone as if to make sure it was a phone before she hung up and located them, the two nice guys running the lot.

Soberly, they took in her story, her voice assured and aiming to please. When she held the slate gray sweater out to Luke, Darrin said "Hey, lady," and held up his hand in a stop gesture to let her know it was his show. "You think we're running a lost and found department here?" His voice was deep and accusatory.

She was clearly taken aback. Her terrier growled a familiar, nasally growl that hit Luke in the stomach. Junie's dog, Murk, was still at home with Luke's mother in Rhode Island, though she was threatening to give it away. Murky's ears perked up and he whimpered pathetically when she said his sister's name. She avoided saying it. They both did. "So what's a dog," his mother said the last time he'd gone to see her. "It's not just any dog," he'd said, scratching hard behind Murk's ears to stave off his whimper as he said, "It's Junie's dog." Someday soon he'd just go get him—ignore his apartment's no-dogs lease.

The woman in the orange raincoat gave it another try. "The man on the phone said he parks here all the time, that you'd be glad to do this for him."

When Darrin asked if she got his name, she said, no, but—

"Look around," Darrin said, "you see any place to stash our customer's belongings, if indeed he's even been in this lot." He turned to Luke. "You seen this sweater before?"

Luke said not me, but that it looked about his size. As he reached for the sweater, the woman stepped back fast on to the terrier's foot. It let out a yelp.

Darrin threw Luke a disgusted look, then said to the woman, "See what I mean, I can't be responsible for no sweater when I got all these cars under my care and my partner here is wanting a new wardrobe."

"I can't just put it back," she said. The sweater hung from her hand like a drowned cat. Luke felt a little sorry for her. Finally Darrin peevishly let her leave it behind. But clearly her faith in humanity had been shaken.

The next person to answer the phone rescued the sweater and walked the fifteen yards to their booth, then got suspicious when Darrin told him, yeah, there's some Tennessee mother—he said mothah—who was sending sweaters to far more people in Boston than they could help. And oddly the sweaters all looked—here he dramatically pointed at the sweater—gray and ratty just like that one. The guy squinted at the phone on their counter then over to the bank of phones. "Man, that is good, really good. Hey, I'll put the sweater back out there and you can do it again." They had an appreciative audience for two more calls that night.

Two or three times a week, when they weren't in class, Darrin and Luke took turns parking cars and tending the gates. Vince and his silver Porsche showed up from time to time to raid the till. Luke still talked about dropping out of design and going on the road. He'd take Junie's dog and keep a journal like she had, maybe work a couple years in the Alaska canneries. Or head for Burning Man in Nevada. Stop at little back road museums—The Hall of Flame Museum full of restored red fire trucks, or the Frog Fantasies Museum in Arkansas, with its frog light beer bottles and frog pipes. "Man, that'll ruin your aesthetic. Damage your eye," Darrin said. Some studying got done, some drawings, too, when the compass or T-square wasn't mislaid. They talked about their ex-girlfriends—Darrin's mother telling him before she died to "marry black." They assessed the other people in their class for talent and drive. Often, Darrin described new inventions he'd found on the web. "Every invention creates a new market for new products," Darrin said. "Computers spawned a whole new office furniture industry." One slow night, he insisted they draw up plans for a better two-man, parking-lot booth.

"We got all this space in front and behind, but no elbow room." He thumped Luke's sketchbook. "Go for it," he said. "The booth of the future. It'll be a competition. Just us two."

Fuck the future, Luke thought. Since his sister's leukemia he wasn't living even one day at a time, he was sleepwalking through each day, hearing his professors—and Darrin—as if from the last row in class.

"And why does the roof's peak go that direction?" Darrin was standing outside by the gate now. "Outhouses have a better aesthetic than this cube."

Darrin took to stopping by Luke's apartment after work and they'd go through a six-pack talking shop, Darrin running his mouth nonstop. "Water coolers need softer lines," he said. He cited things he wanted to redesign, like flashlights, chairs, and water coolers, probably causing Luke's recent nightmares. In one dream, Junie kept rearranging the furniture in her hospital room while the room itself got larger and larger. Luke had to search for her at the beginning of every visit. In another dream, everything in Luke's apartment became something else: the toaster turned into a chair, the chair a lamp, the lamp an eating utensil—the bed was next in line for transformation when Luke jerked awake, sweating. But he was glad for Darrin's recent company. For the first time in months, Luke washed all the dishes and did a mountain of laundry—not that he'd gone so far as to put it all away. But Darrin would be amused that he considered him someone to clean for. Luke's last relationship ended while Junie died. One night, he and Carol had been standing outside of Junie's room while a nurse adjusted her morphine drip, his sister so weak now that she could no longer turn her head, and Carol had caught his naked look of "why her and not you." Recoiling from him, she said, "I can't help it that I'm not the one dying," and he'd slapped her. She slapped him harder, not holding back as he had. He left her there, in the hallway, unwilling to share his grief, ashamed at how alive and powerful his anger had made him feel.

Late one evening after work, while Luke was folding all the laundry he'd saved up, Darrin wandered around his apartment and stopped in front of a photograph of Junie putting together a wooden puzzle Luke had designed for Preston's Three-Dimensional Puzzle course. "Girlfriend?" said Darrin.

So Luke told him about his sister. How Junie was dead eight months after being diagnosed and two months before her high school graduation. How his mother and he took turns sleeping in her hospital room that last week. But he didn't tell Darrin how she'd complained about the way the bed table worked, or rather didn't work. He was afraid Darrin would make it their next project. "See, see," she'd said, twisting her smooth head to indicate the table's bulky inaccessibility behind her. "That dumb table is always out of reach. It doesn't fit beside the bed. It should be on a leash like a dog." Instead he told Darrin that when Junie did sleep, in between her feverish bouts of planning his future, he drew her hands. He sketched them lying beside her on the bed, or smoothing salve on her cracked lips, or fanning her damp face with a get-well card, but they were never right.

"The night she died," he said, "I knew she was dying. Her hands were already growing cool and I traced the left one on the back of an envelope from school." He reached for his sketchbook, pulled out a large white envelope and dropped it on the coffee table.

Darrin leaned forward and placed his own dark hand on top of Junie's outline. Flexing his fingers against hers, he said, "No one—no one will ever design a better hand."

Two nights later, business slow, twelve cars in the lot, Darrin said, "Jesus, those glasses got to go," his attention caught by a man strolling toward the phones, still wearing mirror sunglasses though it was past eight. "Tell me. Where would glasses be without ears," Darrin said. Then, he told Luke, "You make the call this time." Earlier, Luke had watched with mild curiosity as Darrin placed the sweater further away from the phones than usual.

On Luke's third ring Sunglasses stopped, looked around, and ambled over to the phone. Luke almost hung up, but Darrin poked him hard, and finally he went into Darrin's spiel, lamenting his lost sweater—slate gray. As the man spotted it, Darrin nudged Luke again, whispering "give me a minute" then took off out the back of the lot.

"Yeah, it's here. Someone hung it over the fence," Sunglasses said.

So Luke told him it was a graduation gift from his mother in Arkansas, and described her impending visit with her new, fifth husband. Then, hey, he got an idea: Sunglasses could leave it with the guys in the parking lot booth. The man swiveled his sunglasses to where Luke was sitting—Darrin-style—his hand hiding the phone.

That's when Darrin appeared from around the corner. Sunglasses and Luke both watched as Darrin lifted the sweater off the fence and held it up to his skinny chest like he'd found gold. "See the parking lot booth?" Luke repeated. "Leave it there."

"Yeah, well, I don't know—" the man said to Luke.

Luke, relentless, said, "What don't you know?"

Sunglasses slowly turned away from Darrin and cupped his hand over the receiver to whisper, "Some black man just came by and picked it up."

Just then Darrin sauntered over. Luke heard him ask Sunglasses, "Hey, man, this ain't your sweater, is it?"

When Sunglasses said, "No, not exactly," Darrin said, "Then what you think? I got me a new sweater?"

Luke said, "Fuck that," and the man looked startled. "Tell him take it to the guys in the booth."

"Ah—you tell him." Sunglasses held the phone out to Darrin.

Darrin shrugged, "Nah," and tossed him the sweater, then disappeared around the corner.

Sunglasses held the sweater as if it was wired, but his step grew more assured as he approached the booth. Lounging against the gatepost, he recounted for Luke the story of his bravery in wresting the sweater away from some big black man.

"Big black man?" Luke said. "Shoulda let him have it. Think we run a lost and found department?"

The man straightened up like he'd been shot. "Come on. The guy on the phone said you'd know him." Then he spotted Darrin coming across the lot toward them.

"Yo, Luke," Darrin said, hitching up on the booth's other stool. Then to the man, "Hey, you still got that ratty sweater?"

Sunglasses removed his shades and squinted Darrin into sharper focus. "Punks," he said. "Goddamn punks." He dropped the sweater on the pavement and huffed away.

"Okay," Luke said, "It's my turn to steal the sweater."

"Nah," Darrin said. "It won't be any fun. No one's going to be afraid of you."

"I outweigh you by fifty pounds," Luke said.

"So? You're also two inches taller," Darrin said, sticking out his skinny chest. "But you, my man, aren't black."

Darrin was right; it wasn't the same. It was just Luke out on the street, mooning over the sweater while the jerk holding the phone obediently relayed Darrin's message about his sentimental mother and how a missing sweater might break her heart.

•

At Luke's apartment later that evening, Darrin said, talking what he called 'black talk,' "I need to take advantage of what I got. And what I got scares a lotta white folk. I can't be redesigned so I guess it's them that needs the lesson." He was gleeful at being called "some big black man." "I'll really be grooving when someone calls me a 'big black muthah-fucka' and then they see skinny ole me. Don't tell me looks don't count," Darrin said, pointing his beer bottle at Luke. "We're in the looks business." He described an article he'd read about engineers who'd developed a self-contained human heart that was almost ready to be implanted in a human recipient. It needed a big chest because it was bulky, a box really. But the main problem was that the possible recipients thought the heart was ugly, which dismayed the engineers because that sort of poor attitude could adversely affect their heart's success rate. So the engineers sent it over to design guys. "You understand, they gave it to design as a last resort," Darrin said, dangling his empty beer bottle. "Well, design studied their ugly box of a heart and also the human heart, and when they revised the specs on the engineers' heart they made it look more real. Turned out it not only looked better, it worked better. It was a beauty of a heart. They need us, man. Invention needs design."

Luke went to the fridge for two more beers. He didn't know hearts from boxes. What he knew was the human lymphatic system, the paths along which lymph fluids sluice deformed cells that go on to multiply and kill. Doctors didn't need to redesign the lymph system—and finding a cure for cancer was eons away—they just needed to threaten, warn, get it to negotiate. Luke wished he could have told his sister's cancer: she dies, you die.

A week later, Luke's plan for going on the road fell apart when his car was broken into and the back window smashed for a lousy CD player and a leather jacket. Darrin commiserated, saying "Plastic could keep it dry for a while." He studied the car a bit longer then peered over at the pay phones. "See the Ford and Toyota at the two meters in front of the phones?" he said to Luke. "When one of them leaves we move your car in. Don't ask; you'll see why."

Vince had already come and gone, so Darrin sent Luke to idle at the corner and wait for an empty meter. When the Toyota pulled out, Luke slid his car in and fed the meter seven quarters, sadly eyeing his missing back window.

Inside the booth, Darrin was finishing a design for a chair—"got to give that ugly Eames a little competition." He dialed their phone. By now, they'd come to think of it as their phone; both knew the number by heart. When Luke said that with so many cell phones walking around the days of their scam were numbered, Darrin scoffed, "Come May, we'll be out of here and on our own, designing those phones. To hell with your road trip. Now listen up."

A woman carrying a bulging briefcase answered, and Darrin reeled off his newest story: he'd been forced to leave his car on the street 'cause the lot was full and he just needed to know that his girlfriend's new TV was OK. "Bronze," he said. "A '78 Buick." He was at the dentist's he said, with one more cavity to be filled. (He talked as though his mouth was half numb.) So could she just set his mind at ease and check on the car and the TV. Also, he'd tucked four quarters under the left windshield wiper. Would she do him a big favor and put those in the meter too?

"I'll see," the woman said dubiously, even though she was looking right at Luke's car. She extended the phone cord as far as she could, then peered in the broken back window, to where there was no sign of the girlfriend's TV. Back at the phone she said, "I'm afraid I have some bad news."

"I'm afraid I have some bad news." Luke had been with Junie at the hospital when they were given her prognosis. Her eyes had blazed and she had squeezed Luke's hand tighter and tighter as the doctor talked. Their mother cried into a blue handkerchief that had once belonged to their father. Afterward, at home, Luke sat against the wall in his sister's bedroom and watched as Junie gathered up everything she wanted him to have. "Lukie, you won't ever give this away," she said about his first attempt at a ceramic plate. Junie.

After hearing the "bad news" about the missing TV, Darrin would exclaim that surely it couldn't be true, he'd only had one tooth filled and would they look again. Amazing how many people did just that, as if Darrin's persuasively doubting voice on the phone made them also doubt what was in plain sight. Everyone forgot to feed the meter as requested, except one guy who put two quarters into the meter and smartly pocketed the other two.

At least twice a week, they moved Luke's car into the lot overnight and back out on the street the next evening. People continued to answer the phone and report the broken window and missing TV with varying degrees of sorrow and exhilaration.

"You make the call tonight," Luke told Darrin, somehow needing to raise the stakes. "Keep your eyes on the prize." He waited till Darrin started dialing, then he wove through the parked cars and into the alley behind the lot.

Soon Darrin had a man in jogging shorts peering into the back seat of the Buick for the TV and returning to the phone to report the loss. It was at this moment that Luke crept around the fence corner, his arms out bat-like, and proceeded to reach into his already pillaged car and extract two empty shopping bags of his mother's from Neiman's and Saks. He was creeping away when Jogging Shorts must have gotten his instructions from Darrin. "You. Outta there," Jogging Shorts called to Luke, his thumb aiming to spoil Luke's plans. Then he started swatting at Luke as if he were a fly. A nuisance. Some nut. Luke dropped the bags onto the sidewalk and retreated around the corner.

At the booth, Darrin was hysterical, his thin frame electric with energy. "Man, that is so cool. But it's no fun with you doing it. We need a big bad black man on the scene."

"Shit. When you're talking normal in your usual prep school accent, you're as white as I am," Luke said.

Darrin snorted. "You got to be kidding. Man, if you think that, you ain't been playing my game."

"What game?" said Luke.

"Now watch the pro," Darrin said and started off.

Luke grabbed his arm. "Don't do it," he said. "It's dangerous. It's not a game."

Darrin easily pulled free. "Dial." Then he headed out of the lot.

Luke should have let the guy in the bowling jacket go by. He should have waited for a real estate salesman, a pharmacist, a nurse. He should have left town six months ago.

The man picked up right away. "What?" he said. Just that: "What?"

It threw Luke off. The first sentences of his spiel were ragged till he hit the part about his girlfriend's TV.

"Yeah, the car's here. It has a busted window and the TV's missing." To the point. Darrin must have hesitated because Luke had extra mini-seconds to fill before Darrin came creeping around the corner. Bowling Jacket actually watched Darrin creep by.

"You still there?" Luke asked to break his trance.

Bowling Jacket didn't answer, but kept the phone to his ear—held there as if it were a decoy. Finally, he said to Luke, "What?" Then, "Hold on." He let the phone swing free and swiveled to watch Darrin, whose arms emerged from the car dangling with the expensive shopping bags just like Luke's had minutes before.

"Drop it," Bowling Jacket yelled. His gun came from nowhere. "Drop them bags now."

Luke threw down the booth's phone and yelled, "Let him go. Don't shoot. Let him go." He jumped over the gate and onto the sidewalk. Running, he called out, "Those bags got nothing in them."

"Back off, white boy," Bowling Jacket said, his gun still pointed at Darrin.

"I know him," Luke screamed. "We work at the lot. It's a joke."

The man turned to Luke, eyes squinting beneath his red headband. "Fuck with me?" he said, catching Luke's wrist with the butt of the gun.

Almost blind with pain, Luke clutched his arm to his chest, but he could still see the man lunge at Darrin, who danced backwards, arms flailing, empty bags swinging wildly. Then his foot slipped off the curb, bags flew, and he went down, his head hitting the Buick's silver bumper hard.

"No," Luke screamed.

"Joke's on you," Bowling Jacket said. Then he was moving off as a crowd formed around Luke, who was kneeling, willing Darrin to say something, cradling his head with his good arm. Darrin's eyes were wide, staring, in immense and frightening pain.

In a different hospital from Junie's, but seated beside an identical bed, Luke watched as Darrin's mind and body made a slow journey to recovery—the reverse of Junie's swift descent. Almost. Darrin couldn't move his legs, couldn't feel his legs. Luke went to the hospital every day, Darrin's father every night, a tall, grey-haired black man questioning Darrin's doctors with the same precision he no doubt used in court. Doctors were standing at attention when he was done with them. To Luke he said, "You boys were looking at assault charges. Playing a man like that. Boston juries have their own brand of lynch laws." Darrin rolled his eyes at Luke, saying *see where I get it*, then told his father, "Next time leave your briefcase and courtroom lectures at the office and bring us beer."

Luke was there when the doctors gave Darrin the "bad news" line. It preceded their analysis of just how long it might be before he'd walk again, if ever—and then probably with a cane. "Fucking can't improve on a cane's design," Darrin said, his face the color of wet asphalt. He ignored Luke the rest of his visit, staring instead at a football game on his roommate's TV high on the wall, though the curtain was pulled closed between them.

Luke was fired. Vince had one word for them: dumb. Darrin signed the paperwork for taking a leave of absence from school, but only after Luke threatened that if Darrin dropped out, he'd drop out too, go on the road even with a busted window. Go south, find a state with no rainfall. Take the bus and leave the driving to them.

"Shut up. I'll sign the fucker," Darrin said.

Drafting class sent an emissary, Pete Hanley, with a green plant that Luke watered. "You have to soak it good, then throw out the extra water from the container's base," Luke said, reading the instructions.

"Ditch it," Darrin said. "What am I, a captive plant-waterer?"

•

Next time Luke arrived, Darrin wasn't in his room, but he'd left a note at the bottom of his bed. "L. Gone for x-ray. Check the morgue. D."

Luke gave the plant a bit more water, pinched off the dead leaves, then moved it to the windowsill for some natural light. Hospitals were all the same—disinfectants, human detritus, steam-table food. Things clattering by on wheels. The TV looming high on the wall across from the bed, metal plugs and outlets for this and that, the wide door for easy removal to the operating room or morgue, or merely a short jaunt for x-rays of a damaged spine. It was all too familiar—the sagging visitor's chair, the same kind of tri-part metal bed in which Junie died.

Hidden by the curtain, Luke hitched up onto the bed where Darrin would soon be arranged. He stretched out his legs on the thin white sheet, and leaned back to feel what his sister felt: Junie dying, but not yet. Determined, curious, he felt around for the controls. Just as she said, he practically had to lean out of bed to reach the goddamn bedstand—square, stolid, and almost out of range. No leash. He pulled hard at a corner and it slowly rolled toward him, hampered by the phone's cord till the phone crashed to the floor.

"What the hell," the man behind the curtain said, and Luke apologized.

The mattress was so high that he would have to get off the bed to retrieve the phone, but this was difficult to do because he'd ratcheted up the knee part of the bed and now the control box was missing.

"Lukie," Junie had said, in what was to be her last week. Her grin was faint, but still there. "Do you remember, when you got to junior high, how you badgered me and Mom to call you 'Luke'? You wouldn't answer to anything else, and we finally learned." He'd nodded and she asked with flat, urgent finality, "Do you think I'd ever have become a 'June'?" She was serious. Eyes feverish, she wanted to know.

"Do you want to be 'June'?" he finally said, tracing her freckled fingers with his own. When she didn't answer he said, "June," then louder, "June" for her to hear. It was a tiny part of what she wouldn't ever know. Wouldn't ever wear—blue velvet gloves with sequins at the wrist. But sadly, Luke could imagine exactly when she would have become "June." When some boy or man renamed her, whispered "June," before or after they made love for the first sweet time, and then thereafter. A man laying claim, and her bestowing it. June. Oh, Junie.

Luke picked the phone up as if it were a weapon and slammed it onto the table, then he shoved the squat table back against the wall.

"Hey," the curtain said.

Luke needed to get out of there.

On the way to the lobby, he stopped at a bank of bleakly silent phones, daring one to ring. He punched in Darrin's number and waited. Not back yet. Two coffees and a pounding walk around the hospital's grounds later, he tried the number again. Darrin answered on the seventh ring. Luke imagined him turning in the bed, swearing, stretching to reach the goddamn phone.

"So, you'll design wheelchairs," Luke said.

"Where the hell are you?" Darrin said.

"Five, six, maybe seven years from now I'm going to get a Cooper-Hewitt Design Award for a bedstand," he said. "And you, my man, will get second place, tenth place with your wheelchair because your heart wasn't in it."

"I'm hanging up," Darrin said.

"My ass." Luke pictured the effort it would take for Darrin to reach the table so he could slam down the phone, his torso twisting, legs dragging the sheet, a fumbling, futile movement that would convert his pain to rage. "You can't reach that damn table, can you?" Luke asked.

"You gotta do better'n that," Darrin said. But he didn't hang up.

In the long silence, Luke breathed deeply, his cheek wet against the receiver.

"Get your ass back here," Darrin said. "And before you do bedstands, start with bed pans. Something's really wrong that Junie and I have to shit and piss in the same goddamn metal dish."

"I'll be there," Luke said. Glad that, finally, the pressure was on.

Slides

"THE PRODIGAL RETURNS," FRAN'S husband says, greeting her at the door. Coffee mug in hand, Doug gives her a fast, one-armed hug the kids probably think is natural. She sees him trying to read her expression, but she purposely doesn't have one. A "Welcome Home Mom" sign is stuck to the screen as if she's been away for months instead of five days.

"Surpri—ise," Jill and Markie yell, hugging her fast. Then, one on each arm, they pull her into the living room where the slide projector is set up for a show. Markie, still at top volume, says it's just like the movies as Jill yanks shut the drapes.

A row of four chairs sits with the stiff alertness of a jury. Fran would prefer the couch, but Jill insists on the chairs, saying this way it's more like a real movie theater. Markie plugs in the popcorn popper precariously balanced on the piano bench. "He carried it in himself," Jill brags. Clearly this show has brought them to a truce of sorts. Fran hopes it lasts long enough for Doug and her to call their own truce. "The lid!" Jill yells as the first kernel explodes.

Doug pours more scotch into his mug—his second, third?—and asks if Fran would like a drink. She checks to see how many slide trays are on the program—Jesus, four. Yes, she tells him. She drops into a chair and nudges off her heels, wishing she could miss this rerun of chaotic birthday parties, boozy vacations at their endangered lake, scrawny Christmas trees, dead pets. But the kids never tire of these frozen monuments. At the piano, Jill and Markie hover impatiently while the popcorn stages its own small war. Finally its cannonade diminishes and bowls are filled.

"Let's get this show on the road," Doug says, handing Fran a glass of wine. He retrieves his mug then sits beside her in the chair with arms—"The King's Chair," he calls it. Markie hikes up onto her lap and she turns him around and settles him snugly against her chest.

"Here goes." Jill turns on the ancient projector and the screen glows white.

"And there you are," Jill announces as the first slide clicks into place.

And there she is: in her wedding dress. The happy, hopeful bride.

"Oh Jilly," Fran says, trying not to cry, pressing her nose into Markie's hair. He twists around to face her. "Happy Birthday!" he yells to approximate the excitement he assumes she must have felt.

"It wasn't her birthday," Jill says authoritatively. At eight, she already has Fran's habit of talking with her hands on her hips. Markie, five, probably thinks all women do this. Jill returns to her story. "Dad told us all about how you got poison ivy the week before the wedding. You really peed in a poison ivy patch? Used leaves to wipe yourself?" A good story-teller, Jill shivers in sympathy and Markie giggles and clutches his crotch.

"I explained how we were playing tennis and the park johns were locked," Doug says, clearly annoyed. Fran's skin prickles as Jill recites how Fran had to smear icky cream all over her body and wrap herself in a sheet. What was missing in Doug's account is how they still managed to make love in the desperate tangle of damp sheets.

"I can't see the poison," Markie complains.

"Not 'poison,' 'poison ivy,'" Jill corrects him. "It was under her wedding dress."

"It was mostly gone by the wedding," Fran assures them.

On the screen, she is looking straight at the camera—at her father who took the picture just after her mother adjusted the bridal veil. It was attached to what her mother dryly called a "crown of thorns." Her father's revenge for this remark was to leave her mother out of the picture except for an arm.

"Where did you find the slides?" she asks the kids, but she is looking at Doug.

"In the storage room." He shrugs, denying any complicity in this event, but Fran doesn't believe him. She pictures Jill and Markie finding the slides in their fancy silver box and announcing they hadn't seen these before. Doug could have said they were accounting forms, anything, or suggested going to the park. She pictures the three of them lined up on the couch eating KFC chicken while she and Doug get married over and over. He should have warned her. Holding Markie's head still with the palm of her hand, she takes a mouthful of cool wine. Swallows twice.

"That is the beautifullest wedding dress," Jill says, still entranced with the bride on the screen. "Mom, where's your wedding dress?"

"Dad wouldn't let us look for it," Markie tattles.

"That's right," Doug says, scoring a point Markie didn't intend him to have. Fran is grateful the dress no longer exists. She imagines them insisting she put it on for their show, the long train wound carefully around her chair, scraggly flowers from the garden in her lap, watching the slides through the dotted veil. She tells Jill that the wedding dress got left behind several moves ago. Then she thinks to ask, "What were you two doing in the storage room?"

Jill says "nothing" and Markie says "playing."

"They were fooling around while I was in my workshop," Doug says. "You weren't here so—"

"Douglas, stop. You know I needed to go to that conference," she says.

"Jesus. I said they were downstairs with me because you weren't here. Don't make it such a big deal."

"Quiet," Markie says, kicking sideways at his father. "No fighting, Dad. You promised."

Jill clicks the forward button and now Doug and she are standing in front of the church with his parents, whom she'd met for the first time that week. Doug has his mother's red hair and his father's prejudices— the one receding as the other gradually emerges.

"There's grandma," Jill says. "She was alive then." Markie doesn't remember her. Instead he wants to know what the big building is. "A church," Doug says, leaving a lot out. Markie asks what's a church?

Sheepishly, Fran thanks God that the picture changes as Jill says, "Mo—om. Look." She gropes for Fran's arm, eyes on the screen. "Here you are at the wedding. Look at all the candles and flowers." Bouncing, Markie wants to know who got to light the candles?

"An altar boy about twenty years older than you," Doug says into his mug of scotch. "Now watch the show."

"Is this where you and Dad say 'I do'?" Jill asks.

How does she know these things, Fran wonders. The kids have never been to a wedding—and none of their friends' parents are divorced, never mind remarried. Too much TV? She tells Jill these pictures were taken after the wedding ceremony, that they were only posing. "They make it look like the real thing, Jilly, but the actual wedding is over."

"So how was the trip?" Doug's tone is casual.

"Well, it made things clear," she says. It's not what he wanted to hear, but it has to be what he expected.

"Clear." His laugh is a snort, setting into motion the empty mug dangling from his fingers like a pendulum. He lets it drop to the carpet. Only because it's empty.

Jill clicks fast through the next pictures, disgusted with the fake ceremony. Then she stops to back up one slide. "Here's where Dad puts the wedding ring on Mom's finger," she narrates for Markie. Now Fran and Doug are standing at the altar with their backs to the pretend audience—or rather congregation—that is milling around outside the church in a steamy July sun.

"Do you want more wine?" Doug asks. Fran shakes her head no.

"Quiet," Jill says. "Mom, see the little girl in the pink dress. Dad said she carried your wedding ring on a satin pillow all the way down the aisle."

Markie's fingers are slippery with butter as one by one he spreads Fran's bare fingers. "Hey, where's your ring?"

She tells him to shush and squeezes him hard around the waist, wiping her fingers on his shirt. On the plane, on the way home, she took off the wide gold band and dropped it into the pocket of her briefcase. Doug has the grace not to look away from the screen.

In the next slide they are kissing, her halo of veil floating above and around their chaste, fake kiss. Markie makes squishy fish-lip sound effects and Jill tells him to shut up. Finally, the wedding party is assembled on the church steps as if before a firing line. They squint into the sun, hungover from too much champagne at the wedding rehearsal. Hours before the rehearsal, her parents had stood by, alarmed, as she and Doug had a portentous argument because she wouldn't stop vacuuming to make him a sandwich. Doug, divining the future more clearly than she, took off for what stretched into several hours—the tires of his new Saab screeching. Finally, but not chastened, he returned to say, "In my house I will be king." She thought he was kidding, but sure, she said, of course. The next day she married a king.

Six more slides click by fast. Now Doug and she are hurrying down the sidewalk flanked on either side by relatives and friends. Then she is cradling her flowers, gathering the train of her gown, bending forward to get into Uncle Walt's new Buick.

"Look at all the rice," Jill says, and Markie squeals at the blurred fireworks of rice raining on their heads. Fran closes her eyes. Belatedly she read that rice is fatal to birds, expanding until their stomachs explode. She imagines a sea of dead birds floating in her bridal wake.

"Intermission," Doug says imperiously, stooping to pick up his mug from the carpet.

"No." Markie's sneaker just misses Doug's ear.

Fran tells him to stop kicking and gives him a hard bounce.

"Da—ad. We always have to wait for you," Jill says.

"Jilly, be patient," Fran says, also talking to herself.

As Doug crosses in front of the screen to pour himself more scotch, the picture is momentarily projected onto his white t-shirt and she is briefly bowing to him. Too bad he can't see it. Returning with a freshened scotch, he says "you're a little shit" to Markie and pulls his chair out of range of Markie's shoes.

"Please. Don't start now," Fran says softly.

"Why not, Dad's back," Jill says. "Get ready, Markie. Here's the cake with the teensie-tiny bride and groom on top." Behind the mountain of cake, as if in ambush, Fran is holding a long, lethal-looking knife trimmed with an enormous white bow. Doug's hand is firmly guiding hers.

"Yum-yum." Markie jumps down and runs to the screen to take a swipe at the stiff icing. The screen teeters on its flimsy tripod but settles upright. On tiptoe now, Markie tries to reach the tiny groom and Jill screams, "Move!"

"You can't even behave for your mother's first hour home," Doug yells. He picks up a squirming Markie and retreats to his seat. "So it's over," Doug says to Fran, his chin resting hard on Markie's red hair. "Just like that."

Jill swings around to him, her mouth trembling, to say "Da—ad, you know there's more."

Fran tugs on her fuzzy braid. "What's next?" she asks her hopeful daughter. "I forget what comes next." To Doug she says, "You're wrong. It's not over 'just like that.' We gave it years."

"I know," he says, sighing.

The next slides are people sitting at tables, eating something Jill says she can't make out. She goes through them fast then stops. "Here's where you and Dad are dancing." Suddenly, she points to Markie. "The music, Dumb-Dumb. You forgot the music."

"It's too late," Doug says. "It's too late for music." But Markie flies out of his lap and heads for the CD player. Fran bends to pick up an empty popcorn bowl, shielding her face. If it is the Wedding March she will surely weep. Instead a Mozart symphony sweeps through the room at gale force and Jill yells for Markie to turn it down, hands covering her ears. Markie crawls back onto Fran's lap and she is grateful for his weight keeping her there.

"Here's where you throw your bouquet, Mom. But where are you standing?"

Fran peers at the blurred screen, determined not to sniff. She explains that they are back at her house and she is standing on the porch just before they are ready to leave for—she can't say "honeymoon."

"Where are you going?" Markie asks.

"Their honeymoon, stupid," Jill says.

Still trusting her, Markie asks if they went too?

"You weren't even born yet," Jill says meanly.

Markie's shoulders heave. "You suck," he says to her.

"Sweetie, it was before both you and Jill were born," Fran says so he won't think the three of them went on some wonderful trip without him.

"Move it along." Doug's voice is thick with emotion.

"There you are getting into the wedding car," Jill says. "Then you left. On your honeymoon." Markie claps his hands in applause, thinking he recognizes another happy ending. Then, turning, he demands that Fran clap too. She is exhausted, yet it is only the beginning.

When Jill clicks past the last slide the white screen blinds them all—all except Jill, who starts backwards. "Wasn't that great, Mom. You want to see them again?"

"Show's over. That's it," Doug says fast. He tells them to go outside and play and stands to stretch elaborately. "Your mother and I have to talk."

"Da—ad. Just cause you've seen it three times yesterday. It's Mom's turn." Jill turns to Fran, tears in her eyes as if she feels something shift and waver beyond her control. She wants to believe in the slides and so she pleads, "Don't you want to see them again?" but Fran can't do it for her. "Later, Jilly. That was a beautiful show." She gives each kid a fierce hug, her arms straining to conceal what she can't tell them yet.

Jill leans back to gaze up at her. "Were you surprised?" she asks.

"Were you were you were you?" Markie singsongs.

Fran can manage two words. "Totally surprised," she says.

"Outside," Doug yells. "Now."

Jill grabs Markie's hand and drags him to the screen door where he gives her a push through to the porch. Together, they carom into the back yard. Fran catches the door before it slams shut and stands there, watching them through the grey mesh of the screen. When she and Doug tell the kids, will they be surprised? Clearly, they won't understand for a long time, but when they're older she'll remind them of this day. How they did all they could. She will tell them they really tried.

Scenography

HER JOURNAL WAS STOLEN.

More accurately, her car was stolen; the journal was in the trunk. It happened three weeks ago, the day after she made the eight hour drive from Portsmouth to Pennsylvania to spend Thanksgiving with her mother.

She had just broken off a lingering love affair—changed her locks, and packed her lover's clothes, books, CDs, and old x-rays from a surfing accident, and sent them FedEx to Nashua where he taught economics. Keys and locks were intimate objects for her. She always felt moved whenever she inserted a key into a new lover's lock or heard her own bolt slide back from the twist of a lover's wrist after they had, with studied casualness, exchanged keys. In her journal she kept a list of men who once had her key—Harry's name was last.

As a way of steeling herself against Harry's calls to explain his small errors of judgment these past months, she called her mother.

"I don't suppose you'll be coming home for a family Thanksgiving again this year, Ceily," her mother said. She continued to say "family" even though she'd been widowed for ten years and Ceily was an only child.

"I'll be there," Ceily said. "My car is already packed."

Two days later, while she was grocery shopping in Shaw's and trying to decipher her mother's list, the car was stolen. First there was the numb disbelief that she would have to wheel her cart of organic turkey and groceries back into the store and explain, and then dismay that she'd have to call the police and admit she'd left her keys in the car.

They arrived minutes later in full small-town regalia, lights flashing, suits too new, leather holsters showing no signs of sweat. She waited impatiently as they gazed at the pale blue Chevy now parked where her green Subaru had been. The older man did the talking while the young cop listened, nodding.

"Stolen cars in Irwin usually end up borrowed by kids," he said. Then he wrote down her mother's address and phone number and her own out-of-state address. "Anything else missing?"

"Not much. I unpacked everything last night."

"These cars turn up in a day or two, pretty close to home," the older cop said, "though in this case, 'home' being New Hampshire, it ain't likely." The young cop laughed and Ceily looked away, grateful they hadn't asked about keys.

After she carried grocery bags from the taxi into the front hall, wearily telling her mother a story she'd have to retell later, her mother asked if anything else was missing. Ceily omitted the keys, repeated "not a thing," and went out for the last brown bag.

Then she remembered her journal, a worn burgundy leather notebook. She remembered the mean entry describing last night's homecoming—the passages about how she felt being in her old room again with its silly canopy bed and Hollywood dolls on shelves where books should have been, and a list, no less, of things about her mother that annoyed her. Can the sum of little things be a big thing? She could almost reproduce the list from memory: burned oatmeal and mushy vegetables; the church's *Daily Word* heavy with moisture in the bathroom; the two mismatched spots of rouge; veiled references to Ceily's father's gambling; the hypocrisy of medicinal sherry and gin; smoking in spite of doctor's orders; her line "I never thought a daughter of mine would" finished with "not get married," or "leave the church," or "decorate stages—like playing house."

"Nothing's missing," she told her mother with dramatic feigned relief.

On Wednesday, they sat down to a steaming cup of tea before they started drying bread for the dressing and overcooking the cranberry sauce. Ever since Ceily had left for college ten years before, her home seemed increasingly like a stage set. Plastic covers on the lampshades, a row of Readers Digest condensed books held in place by two grey dog figurines, hard rock-maple furniture which long ago had turned a bright orange. If a script ever called for a small-town American living room circa 1990, it would be hard to assemble it more convincingly than this. She'd have to send a van to her mother's home; borrow her bed and dolls, the chrome dinette set and planter coffee table. She regretted that such minor things separated her mother and herself—until her mother asked to hear the story of the stolen car for the third time. She seemed to relish most Ceily's embarrassed explanation to the grocery store manager, her annoyance with the police. Her mother's tongue clucked and her thin lips moved toward her ears—a movement Ceily had too late in adolescence finally recognized as a smile.

All day Ceily avoided thinking about her journal, but that night she missed her usual ritual. A computer entry wouldn't do. Where was her journal now?

She decided: four kids had stolen her car. Two boys and two girls, all with meekly punk haircuts that Irwin would still find alarming, but just a few safe weeks away from a normal comb-out.

First, they would have gone out to the mangy golf course for late night parking, then up to the old strip mine, now the town dump. There, a midnight drag. Tires spun out and the smell of burned rubber mingled with the ashy smell of the newly formed hills. Finally, to the empty graveled lot behind the movie house where the kids abandoned the car within walking distance of the trailer park and three-decker flats in which they lived.

The next day, while her mother and two bridge friends prayed over the singed turkey, Ceily wished the kids an equally successful holiday.

A few days later her car still hadn't turned up. The kids had obviously decided to keep it longer than usual, so she gave rein to their adolescent curiosity. She imagined: one of the boys would open the trunk first, a man's job, and peer around looking for tools, a radio, tires to sell. Her tote bag—red canvas from a cosmetic special—would catch a girl's eye. They'd dump out the contents hoping for exotic perfumes, pills, or lacy underwear—and there would be her journal.

Now what? One girl would take it home to the trailer park where she lived and read it late into the night. The girl would be annoyed by the sloppy handwriting and periodically get up to try a new eye shadow or plaster more Silk on her hair. The next day there would be an improvisational reading at the All-Night Diner while the girl's friends sat around listening. She would express amazement at how she disliked the exact same things about her own mother. Ceily pictured them whispering together, leaning toward each other over thin hamburgers and shiny French fries as if close to the punch line of a dirty joke. She pictured them reading her analysis of how Harry's love-making changed, of how his big hands and feet, which were at first terribly erotic to her, now seemed the appendages of some strange heavy animal. Once, as he slept and before she left for the theater, she stood and looked down at them hanging over the edge of her sheets. It was a little thing to record. But wasn't that what journals were for?

Surely the boys would agree with her rant about their small town where their young souls were bursting with the hope of finding someone over twenty-one to buy their beer and pills and their raunchy expectations of getting laid?

But the journal would stay with the girls. They would read certain passages aloud in turn, giggling as they applied black polish to long fingernails. Certain passages they read when all alone, passing the journal around—finally beginning to realize that sex was supposed to last a good deal longer than two minutes, to also feel good for the girl, and needn't take place in stolen cars. Ceily imagined one of the girls secretly buying a blank book and starting a journal of her own.

At the Greyhound Terminal, Ceily gave her mother's thin shoulders an extra squeeze and kissed her moist spots of rouge. Although these visits also showed Ceily how alike they actually were, still she loved her mother most when leaving her.

Harry called as soon as she returned to Portsmouth. As he talked, she wondered if his ears burned from exposure in the Pennsylvania diner. Ceily found it easy not to listen and finally hung up. What she found hard was not writing in her journal. She'd been prescient in buying a lifetime supply of inserts, but she hadn't considered that the leather binder itself might go missing. Occasionally she used odd pages of stationary and once began a new loose-leaf notebook and a file on her laptop titled IN PLACE OF, but it wasn't the same. In the past, she had settled into her wing chair with a glass of wine or a pot of tea steaming beside her and the journal on her knees. Sometimes only once or twice a week, sometimes daily, she had recorded the ebb and flow of love and work, drew detailed sketches for the sets of plays she someday hoped to stage, made lists of letters to write, places she wanted to go, and people she intended to stop seeing. Now, a lot seemed pent up inside and her next sets for *Mother Courage* were more elaborate than usual. The director complained they would cost too much, but only she knew the real price. Her imagination kept returning to her journal in Pennsylvania: perhaps sensing that time was running out, the girls would reluctantly replace the journal in her red tote bag and the boys would ditch the car. She pictured the old cop nodding his head at his prediction come true, listing her car and its contents on some dog-eared police form just before they asked her mother to sign for it. "I'll call her right away," her mother would say, beaming. Breathless, Ceily rehearsed her lines as she'd watched actors do—changing inflection and emphasis. Because she knew with certainty that her mother could not resist the temptation to read Ceily's assessment of their uneasy relationship and her memories of past family holidays of gluttony and gin. From there she would leaf through the pages looking for passages about lovers and leave-takings, about men Ceily wouldn't marry. Or worse, men who she suspected wouldn't marry Ceily. And Ceily's sketches for various scenes for next season's repertory would confirm for her that Ceily was "still playing with doll houses or moving furniture around like any hired hand." "Mom, it's called 'scenography'," Ceily would say, but her mother still held that Ceily should have been a nurse.

Ceily waited for her mother's call.

But it didn't turn out like that at all.

•

IT WAS A MYSTERY.

Just when he was wishing for a windshield this car turned up, clearly abandoned, with the keys lying on the front seat. The seat wet with the previous night's rain.

He put his backpack and camera bag in the car and then took a few more pictures of the strange strip-mined landscape. He took pictures through the windshield, prismed by a hundred drops of rain. In the city, when the need for a windshield hit him he borrowed a friend's car. But here he felt as if some potential friend had left him her keys.

It knew it was "her" because he found a notebook in the trunk. Ceily Sentry—he liked the sound of her name. He wrote his own name, Ray Clayton, beside hers on the inside cover and positioned it carefully on the dashboard, propped up against the steering wheel. Then he wiped the windshield clean and, using his elbows as tripods, he leaned on the car's hood and snapped a picture of "Ceily Sentry and Ray Clayton."

Trying to remember how long it was since he'd used a jack, he set about changing a flat. Then he thought about the logistics of turning the car in. And he thought about keeping it another day. He weighed the risk of being caught and jailed as a thief.

He decided one more day wouldn't hurt. That night he laid low about fifty miles away from where he'd found it, anticipating the next day's superb light with the weatherman's promise of clear skies and no humidity. He spread out his lenses on the motel sheet and cleaned them carefully, polishing their glass to a high, dense shine.

He'd been obsessed with frames since he'd been given his first camera when he was eight. He wanted to contain things the way his bedroom window contained the brisk busy street four stories below. Outside: fruit stand, butcher shop, newsstand fronting for the local numbers game, three trees he furtively watered in long hot dry spells, a Radio Shack, mailbox, pastry shop, and furniture stores glistening with gold chairs and beaded oil lamps; on top of these stores rose thirty-six floors of apartments like his own. Then there were cars, window displays, people, light, and the change in seasons.

At ten he realized he could take his frames with him if he wore glasses. For the next two months he pretended such bad eyesight that his parents took him to an ophthalmologist who gave him a stern lecture before suggesting he be sent to see Father Garrity. If he'd lived in a different neighborhood, it would have been a psychiatrist instead of a priest who fell asleep halfway through his confession anyway. Finally, at sixteen when some guys were growing shoulder length hair and Grateful Dead t-shirts, his parents began to feel relieved that his politics extended only to clear glasses and they finally ceased caring.

Now, two pairs of clean glasses sat on the bedsheet next to the newly cleaned lenses. Maybe someday he'd move to digital photography, but first he needed to take the Weston/Adams route. His temporary windshield was parked right outside the door. He didn't get around to reading the notebook that first night.

The next day he returned to county roads, maneuvering back and forth to get the angle of the windshield just right before he parked the car. Always he sat in the back seat, focusing from the ledge of the front seat for the first shots. Then the rest from outside, his back leaning on the right front headlight.

He went through seventeen rolls of film. Exhausted, he checked into a different motel and had a sandwich in the adjacent diner. There he met a youngish elderly couple who put Ceily's New Hampshire plates and Portsmouth dealership sticker together with him.

"We've thought of retiring there," the wife said. And when Ray nodded she went on, "It's small and rustic and has nice shops."

Her husband rolled his eyes. "Rustic is what she wants to see. She don't see the ships and heaps of salt and coal. Rusted bridges and empty warehouses."

"It's all there," Ray agreed with both of them and paid his bill.

Back in his room he stretched out for a nap, watching the colors behind his eyelids till he dozed off. He woke wanting to call Helena and then remembered she'd moved out two months before, saying she wasn't ready to settle down. She had shiny straight bangs that framed her face and tilted when she moved her head. He still hadn't developed the last three rolls he'd taken of her.

It was too early to turn in but too late for scouting. He decided to see what Ceily Sentry was up to.

He read backwards.

He met her mother first. He could picture the canopy bed, the sherry or gin hidden in the closet. Her angry description of such a picturesque town. He grinned as daughterly guilt dripped from the page—probably some old maid still caught in her mother's power. His own parents were dead; he missed them. They hadn't read the *Daily Word*, thank god, but they hadn't understood his photographs either. They had asked for an extra copy of his first book and framed their favorites: tiny muted reproductions in plastic frames he'd never had the heart to disavow.

Still reading backwards: interspersed with the text were tiny drawings of doll houses, or rather miniature rooms. But then he read about Harry, self-consciously aware of his own size thirteen boots at the foot of the motel bed. He wanted to like Harry, but reading back through Harry's missed dates and bad economies, he found Ceily convincing him that Harry was well abandoned. In the presumably happy times, there were brief jottings of events and periods of silence for days as she worked "feverishly" on *Mother Courage*.

Then he understood. Those drawings were stage designs, sets for plays. He straightened up and punched his pillow to support his back. Sure, *Three Sisters* was Chekhov, not some family of female dolls. He started from the back of the journal again and stopped at each tiny stage, fascinated by the straight line of the floor, the curbed apron. The drawings—with furniture and pictures—were precise and clean, and always the depth of the stage was there in some straight horizon line that met the backdrop. Then he read on about how she liked working with furniture slightly larger than life because she wanted to pull the audience forward into her sets.

She seemed to have begun the New Year with Harry at a party they "retreated" from early. Her resolutions: lose ten pounds; see less of Harry; use evenings better (stick with one or two glasses of wine); skip the social media; be nicer to Mom. Not sure that Mom deserved it, he flipped forward a few more pages and a piece of paper fell to the floor—a list of men's names. The list felt as if it had been moved from notebook to notebook over the years—how many years, Ray wondered. The handwriting had changed from the first three names: Eric Gerber, Sam Levinson, and Jack Sennott were round and looping and black with light strokes. The next names were all with different pens, and the strokes grew increasingly bolder as the letters straightened and broke off abruptly.

Ray patted his pocket for a pen and rose to search around the motel desk. Just in time he stopped himself from adding his name after Harry's. Then he came across a dog-eared photograph of a young woman caught in the awkward formality of graduation pictures. He liked her large dark eyes, and regretted that harsh light on her long hair. He could imagine a soft shadow across her left shoulder. Wind blowing her hair toward the camera lens.

For the first time she seemed real to him. Ceily Sentry from Portsmouth, New Hampshire. Land of rustic shops and rusty bridges— and Ceily's changing stages. How long had it been since he'd seen a play, felt the lights go down, watched the curtains swing back from the framed lives of characters? It suddenly occurred to him that Ceily was working as seriously with edges as he was.

Her journal had no address, no telephone number. 411 gave him her number. Someone answered "hello" in a sleepy voice.

"Ceily?"

"Yes."

Jesus, he didn't know what to say.

"Who is this?"

Should he say that he'd found her car? That he was on his way? That she was right about Harry?

He hung up firmly to let her know it wasn't a heavy breather. He would sleep tonight and tomorrow be on his way. He hoped she hadn't lost her resolve to break with Harry. And what he'd say when he got there—he didn't know. He simply knew her. He would send her some of his photographs with a note by way of introduction. Then drive north and cross New York to Massachusetts, have the car washed in Boston, check the oil. Do some laundry, catch a haircut. And once again point the car north, let it find its way home.

Ways to Spend the Night

THE FIRST DAY AFTER Carson and his wife checked into Hayes Cape Cabins they had an argument. Now, Carson was holed up in the office, Meadowlark, Cabin 1, listening to the ever-disheartening evening news and Juliet was knitting and sulking in Gull, Cabin 9. All of the cabins were named for birds. It was late October and not exactly meant to be a vacation. When a dark green car turned onto the sandy drive, Carson and his wife still weren't on speaking terms.

The car, its huge engine thrumming, was a large American model Carson didn't recognize—the kind that in a head-on collision always ended up intact and on top. Belatedly, he realized that Mr. Hayes, the cabins' absent owner, had neglected to hang a NO next to the VACANCY sign advertising efficiency cabins with cable TV.

Carson could see the silhouettes of two people, a man and a woman weighing the various amenities of Hayes Cape Cabins against those advertised a few miles back. How could they resist the pots of straggly geraniums squatting on each cabin's steps, or the unlikely cabin aviary, or the enchanted forest of dark looming pines. Why were they here?

The stuffed chair where Carson sat had been molded over the years by Mr. Hayes, who was in Florida, assessing the damage done by Hurricane Ivan to his Tampa Bay trailer park. Hours after their arrival, Mr. Hayes had shown up at their cabin door, somewhat abject, to ask Carson and his wife if they would "mind the store" for him. His nephew, who did the yearly repairs, was unable to come early. Clearly, Mr. Hayes had counted on them to agree—and of course, they had. It gave them another reason to avoid accusations and too-glib confessions of infidelity and betrayal.

Through the thin trunks of the pines, Carson thought he saw the flame of Juliet's red hair in the window of Gull, but he couldn't be sure. That morning, when he had summoned courage from a place still unexplored and said, "We have to talk," she'd said, "Not yet," and stalked out for a mile walk in the woods, on a path worn down years before.

Carson slouched further into the gully of Mr. Hayes' chair to avoid being spotted peering through the window. He considered going out to tell the couple "no vacancy," but it was too obvious that the place was as deserted as an amusement park under quarantine. Besides, keys to all the cabins except cabin 9, Gull, dangled in plain view. If they came in, he'd have to explain the situation: that he didn't own these birds, and couldn't rent them out with the owner away. Please leave, he willed. You don't really want to witness my wife and me killing each other.

The passenger door opened and a woman's shiny, black high-heels sank into the sandy path. Wobbling, she stood on legs that could not be ignored. Her long blouse, maybe it was a short dress, glowed pinkly in the day's weak light. The woman's hair seemed to be pink, too, but surely that couldn't be so. She gazed around expectantly, then set the office bell to tinkling.

"I heard about cabins like these, but I've never actually seen them before except on TV," the woman said in a low, sandy voice. Her smile was beguiling, in spite of—no because of—gleaming, slightly buck teeth that rested on her lower lip like Chiclets. It completely disarmed Carson, who guessed her age as anywhere between twenty-five and fifty. Sadly, anyone could peg him and Juliet at a precise forty-five.

The woman gazed at the tell-tale keys then tiptoed over to the window, looking out on the semi-circle of cabins. "They are like doll houses. Tiny porches. Windows on either side. Exactly what I hoped they'd be."

Carson could only nod. Just before Mr. Hayes left, he shuffled around the office showing Carson and Juliet where things were: cabin keys, outdoor floods, emergency phone numbers, everything in its place with the sense of order that by seventy Carson supposed one finally achieves. Lastly, Mr. Hayes thumped a large, dog-eared reservation pad. "No more reservations on the books, and hardly a soul comes by in the off-off season." When Juliet stepped forward to peer at the reservation page, Carson admired her wariness, which Mr. Hayes chose not to notice. Instead he described the devastation the hurricane had wreaked on his trailer park. Why, Carson wondered, did people build trailer parks in areas constantly threatened by hurricanes? Trailers became missiles the moment the wind came up. "If you hadn't been guests here several times before," Mr. Hayes told them, "I'd have shut the place early. Gone to Florida to clean up the mess and stayed there to hassle the insurance adjusters."

The woman with the Chiclet teeth tapped the window with a pink fingernail and pointed at the cabin furthest back from the road, Sandpiper, Cabin 5. "I think we'll take that one."

"Ah, Sandpiper," Carson said, as if approving of her choice. How to explain that it was only by chance—a result of an argument—that Carson was even in the office. "The thing is—"

When a loud horn sounded, the woman turned and minced birdlike out the door. Seconds later she was in tow behind an enormous man who wouldn't have fit into Carson's Toyota. His solid chin and neck were shades darker than the proverbial shadow and matched his sunglasses.

"Thought I'd speed things up," the man said. "I bet Lolly here already got her cabin picked out. Don't you, baby?"

"I do." The woman—Lolly—pointed at Sandpiper.

"We're not—" Carson began then stopped. Did he really want anyone to know that he and Juliet were alone in this deserted aviary?

"Sandpiper. That right, Lol? Sounds like a bird."

Lolly nodded, happy and somehow sad at the same time.

The man tugged the registration pad out from under Carson's fingers, signed it, then handed the pen to Carson. It said, "Sadow Construction." Then he pulled out a flat wallet and flipped a platinum credit card onto the counter.

The credit card machine, connected to the phone by a shiny black leash, was a mystery that Carson didn't want to try and solve in public. Juliet, he was sure, would have the patience to figure it out. He pushed the credit card back across the counter. "If you will stop by tomorrow, Mr. Sadow—"

"Not Say-dough. It's Sadow—rhymes with shadow," Mr. Sadow said. Then he held out his hand for the key. Unhappily, Carson surrendered it.

"I was forced to decide on the spot," Carson told a smoldering Juliet.

Her back was to him as she peered out their window at Sandpiper. Carson had already noted that Mr. Hayes' "minding the store" wasn't exactly the precise set of instructions it had once seemed. "They're here. It's done," he said. "Unless you want to knock on their cabin door and explain that your husband made a mistake."

"Which one?" Juliet asked. She didn't expect an answer and he didn't have one. When she asked, "So who are they?" Carson said he didn't know, but Sadow was in construction in Connecticut.

"What a tank of a car," she said. "And that blouse. Maybe she thinks it's a dress. I hope you realize that now we can't leave."

"Leave?" he said in wonderment. Together?

Juliet wheeled around. Had he said "together" out loud? "We just got here," he said. "We have over a week to go."

"You're the one who said 'leave' last night," Juliet said. Then dismissing that, she asked, "So how long is the green car staying?"

When Carson admitted he hadn't asked, Juliet said, "I'm going to find that damn NO for the VACANCY sign. Surely Mr. Hayes needed one in high season." And she was gone.

Their most recent argument happened the evening after Mr. Hayes left, when Carson and Juliet had snooped inside the other cabins. "The only perk of this job," Juliet said, rattling a handful of keys. The slanted evening light transformed her curly red hair into a flaming wide-brimmed hat. She was slim, and had once been pliant in his hands.

"Aren't you curious about how different they are?" Juliet said. No— and well, yes, Carson thought, remembering her sister Diedre, then followed her to Osprey, Cabin 2.

Curiosity had been one of his lame excuses for Lisa, the new person in human resources at the software firm where he worked. Their affair hadn't lasted longer than the summer, though it added to the fraught atmosphere of his marriage. Now he and Juliet were here to repair unacknowledged and, Carson feared, unknown wounds.

The cabins were arranged around a sandy semi-circle of a lane, each with its own tiny porch and a parking space for one car. Pushing open the door of Osprey, Juliet set the game in motion.

"OK. On a scale of one to ten." Mold dappled a corner, and twin beds held down wall-to-wall puce carpeting that surely had fleas. Carson gave it a weak two. Tern, Cabin 3, sported an old-fashioned wooden crib and high chair with robin decals. "Vintage decals," Juliet said, "but it's still only a five." Cabin 4, White Owl, was empty except for a rickety wooden stepladder and three red buckets strategically spaced on the floor. "Less than zero," Carson said. Sandpiper, Cabin 5, was the most attractive, with a faded, hand-hooked rug and lumpy quilt. Everything in cabins 6 and 7, Plover and Warbler, even the photograph, Provincetown Dunes—was identical. Blue Heron, Cabin 8, had wicker furniture, a blue-checked tablecloth, blue drapes, and pale blue chenille bedspreads.

"Deidre and I had the exact same bedspreads growing up," Juliet said. "God, how I miss her."

It was an arrow to Carson's heart that Juliet assumed she missed her sister more than Carson did. Lord knows he missed Deidre in his own flawed way. She was the real secret of his storm.

Blue Heron also had a Bennington pitcher that Juliet, over Carson's objections, carried back to Gull to fill with dried flowers. Carson's objections continued when Juliet pushed the couch into a corner, unplugged the TV, and dragged two reading chairs in front of the window. It felt too cozy to Carson, who also feared the reason they were here. "Let's leave," he had blurted out.

"Leave? Leave!" Juliet echoed in amazed outrage, her arms now resting on the reading chair she'd just pushed into place. "You're the one who signed on as Keeper of the Birds." Before collecting her knitting and flouncing into the tiny bedroom, she placed her foot on the chair and sent it flying back into the middle of the room, where it bumped against Carson's weak knees. "We're not leaving. But it's your move."

Toward morning, he woke sweating beside a snuffling Juliet, the word they used for her indelicate snoring. Suddenly, with a vengeance, Carson's nightmare from the last hour blossomed in his mind. In it, Deidre was dying in Mass General Hospital. Juliet was off somewhere and Carson had gone to visit Deidre alone. When he tiptoed into room 312, Deidre was wearing a red-sequined gown that kept snagging on her white hospital blanket. Holding out her thin arms to Carson, she'd announced that she'd made a miraculous recovery and was ready to resume their affair, and oh, how she'd missed him. Her room too had undergone a transformation. Red brocade drapes merged night with day. A wall of bookcases was filled with Carson's favorite biographies. A slim hospital bed sat beside Deidre's own bed, the back cranked up at an angle that in the dream Carson found faintly erotic. "Oh, that," Deidre said waving her hand at the extra bed. "I've ordered a queen-size and a hot tub. We won't have to wait long." Carson remembered being terrified that Juliet was going to appear any moment and discover their affair, and sure enough, her high heels were soon clicking down the hall toward them, her arms full of Carson's clothes. The two sisters watched in their usual complicit amusement as Carson struggled to fit his suits and jackets into the room's narrow metal closet. He realized that they must have flipped a coin for him.

With a tiny dance step and wave Juliet left. Whispering his name, Deidre held out her red-sequined arms to Carson and at that point he'd woken up, chilled and sweating, pathetically relieved that it had been only a dream. He'd peered around Gull, felt the bed flat, double, normal, and filled with his sleeping Juliet.

But Carson's relief drained away as he faced the dream's kernel of truth. It was his affair with Juliet's sister—not his stupid affair with

Lisa—that he regretted most.

It all started with Juliet at work. Deidre staying with them during a brief separation. Her chicken soup ministering to a wretched cold that kept Carson bedridden. Wine in the middle of the day. A conversational impasse. Reaching for her, his hand between her thighs. In the two years that followed, he'd found in Deidre something that was not lacking in Juliet, but in himself. Deidre he could take from, and she was generous toward his childish ardor. Juliet simply didn't see the wimp he was; or maybe she refused to see it. He also discovered that he could love two people at once.

He felt such guilt when Juliet opened her arms to him, when her hands opened him. Nor could he ignore Deidre's sisterly horror at what they were doing, even as they made plans for their next meeting. The toll taken by the emotional chaos of assignations and deceit had been too high: holidays the families spent together when they dared not touch; colognes and perfumes they didn't allow themselves to wear for each other; his pure terror the afternoon when Deidre was late and hadn't called, and he suspected Juliet knew. He and Deidre still loved each other even as they brought it to an end. Relieved of love.

Later, weak and dying, Deidre had made him promise that he would never tell and had made the same promise to him. They'd been alone in her hospital room, Carson seated on her white hospital bed, the back tilted up, her cold hand beneath his. Her voice was whispery, faint. "For Juliet to know, I would have to be here to get railed at, punished—and I won't be. I would have to be here to beg forgiveness and I won't be. Please, I have to trust you." She closed her eyes. He'd tasted tears without salt. She was purest water, air, and soon she would be fire.

"Bad news," Juliet said, coming through Gull's screen door. "The 'NO' is missing." She stood peering out Gull's window. Evening light made a silhouette of her tense back, her wiry hair riding the crest of her strong, freckled shoulders. Carson felt heat. How long since he'd buried his hands in that wiry hair, pulled her to him, kneaded her scalp.

"Here she comes. Lordy, they must think we're the welcome wagon," Juliet said, seconds before Lolly scratched at their screen door. Her pink skirt-blouse had been exchanged for a pea-green jumpsuit. And now her hair looked slightly green.

"Hi there," Lolly said, her nose close to the screen, white Chiclets resting on her full bottom lip. "Hope I'm not interrupting. Hard to believe we forgot a corkscrew."

Even in their small cabin, Lolly resisted standing still. "Oh, I'd love to knit," she said, picking up the red mohair scarf that hung from two needles. "Is it hard to learn?"

Juliet said buy some needles and she'd give Lolly a lesson. Juliet had taken up knitting a year ago—her therapist's suggestion—for stress. Carson understood why Juliet would knit through editorial meetings and the disturbing news from the Middle East, but he resented how Juliet also knitted during their arguments as if they would otherwise be a waste of time. And somehow he couldn't picture Lolly working away on pink or blue booties.

"Size 10 needles," Juliet said, handing over their corkscrew. At the door, Lolly waved a familiar little wave. Smiled her Chiclet smile.

Catching his eye, Juliet said, "Promise me there won't be any more guests," and Carson promised.

The next morning, he went to the office to do his own search for the NO to add to VACANCY, and again was amazed at Mr. Hayes' sense of organization. There were photograph albums of a young Mrs. Hayes with a parrot and several cages of birds. Account books lined one shelf. On a bottom shelf, *Playboy*s were sandwiched between *Sports Illustrated* and *Cape Cod Living*. The girls in the air-brushed centerfolds looked more like life-size, rubber sex dolls than real women with real pubic hair. He felt a stirring. Juliet's red hair sprouted a feathery path he used to lovingly traverse with his tongue from her belly button down. Before Lisa.

The office door tinkled. Sadow had come by to return the corkscrew. In spite of the gray day, he still wore sunglasses, and it seemed likely that his beard was intentional. A disguise?

He set the corkscrew on the counter and asked if the whale watches in Provincetown actually watched whales. "Maybe they're really party boats? Singles stuff. I mean do you have to go on a whale watch with other people?" Outside, the green car's motor was humming with purpose. What purpose?

"Probably, to make it cost-effective," Carson said, adding that he hadn't been on a whale watch for years.

"Money always talks," Sadow said, slapping the counter hard enough to make the corkscrew bounce.

Please leave, Carson wanted to say.

After Sadow left, Carson called Juliet to say he was headed to Snow's in Orleans for a NO and did she need anything? Not a thing. Had Lolly come by for that knitting lesson?

"She doesn't exactly seem like the baby blanket type," Juliet said.

Driving down Route 6, he felt as if he'd been let out of jail.

Two hours later, Carson had the "NO" ready to hang when an ancient Honda coughed its way to the office. Doors slammed and a young man emerged, haggard, thin, with a frayed collar beneath a real beard. He went around to the driver's side to offer assistance to his very pregnant wife. She in turn opened the back door to reach in and release from a car-seat a howling, swaddled baby, with the largest mouth Carson had ever seen. Two tiny front teeth. He wondered if the Sadows had children? Children with Lolly's irresistible teeth.

The office door tinkled again. The young mother, her cheeks glistening with sweat, held her baby tight with love and puzzlement. Their domestic little group filled the office and made Carson feel inordinately happy. He knew he was grinning as he quoted an unbelievably low rate and described the perfect cabin, Tern, number 3, complete with crib and highchair, and a microwave for bottles. The man said, "Great. Great," then, sheepishly, as if it had been an afterthought, the man said, "Uh, we have a dog…"

"A dog. Not a problem," Carson assured him. "I love dogs."

A low-slung spotted mutt emerged from the back seat, and Carson wished it had been larger, more like a guard dog. Its fur and skin were splotchy. Was that smell the baby or the dog? It lay down in the middle of the office floor, and had to be coaxed to leave. "Arthritis. He's old," the young man said.

Carson helped the couple move in to Tern, carrying bags of baby supplies and dog food—all the while hoping the Sadows would find the baby's wails annoying enough to leave.

"Enjoy your stay," he bellowed through Tern's door, which set the baby howling even louder. They were the Beeks, Ginny and Jeremy. And little Oliver Beek.

"You promised no more guests," Juliet accused him when she returned from her walk and heard the racket coming out of Tern. With long swishes, she unlaced her hiking boots and pushed into her clogs. "You're dangerous in that office. You've turned into someone who can't say no."

Ignoring this, he explained that they had spent their honeymoon in Tern, and that she was pregnant, so how could he turn them away. "Their name is Beek. They belong in this aviary." Somehow the young family made him feel unaccountably safe. Forced to put a name on it, Carson would have said safe from Sadow's menace, from something in the shadow of the Sadows' lives.

Juliet's red hair couldn't be tamed by the new Cape Cod baseball cap she pulled on. "I'm taking the car and I'm going to have a divine dinner and a bottle of vintage Bordeaux. And you march right back to that office and choose a key. Six cottages are empty—including the one with the stepladder and buckets. You clearly have a knack for sleeping anywhere."

That night Carson slept alone in Osprey, Cabin 2. All night the baby howled and the dog alternated between whimpering and barking. Carson looked for a light in any of the cabins. Dark. A solid loneliness lay on his heart—shocking in its abrupt appearance, swooping down to take his breath away. Midnight. He wanted to go home. He wanted to go home not with Juliet, but to her. To their past collective life of books and morning sex and cooking smells, their companionable togetherness apart.

Around two a.m., unable to sleep without nightmares, he rose, pulled on his jeans, and stood on his cabin's tiny porch. Throat-thrumming wails were still coming from Cabin 3. How can a baby cry that long? Was it teething? Surely Juliet was awake, too.

He crossed the dewy grass and crept around the side of Gull to Juliet's open window. Juliet was sleeping on her side, naked. He had a fleeting thought—benevolent almost—of her in the arms of another man as the moon made an alabaster figure of her rounded shoulder, her deep, deep waist, her solid hip and thigh. What could lead us back, Carson thought, to simple loyalty and love? Juliet's narrow ankles were primly crossed and caused his heart to lurch, his mind to gently part them.

For the next two days they took turns with the car. One day he went to the used bookstores in Wellfleet, then on to an abandoned P'town, whose summer entrepreneurs had whacked the tourists for their dollars then followed their bank deposits out of town. But he loved the rakish atmosphere they left behind. Real artists and writers, real fishermen, real fish stews. Two other days he took long walks on the ocean beach at McGuire's Landing and out to Indian Neck on the Bay where a gull with a broken leg limped around doing just fine. He missed Juliet's piss and vinegar. Last night, when he'd gone back to Gull for clean clothes, Juliet was sitting in the dark, which startled him. "What are you doing?" he said. Could she knit in the dark?

"Thinking," she said. And to his "About what?" she said "You'll know eventually. Turn out the light when you leave."

For the next few nights, he moved from Osprey to Plover, to Blue Heron, occasionally crossing paths with young Beek carrying the dog into the trees to do its business. Twice, Carson stepped in shit. The dog waggled its long tail when Beek passed Carson on the way back to Osprey, where the young mother must be close to despair. At night, Carson used his pillow to drown out the intermittent cries of the wailing baby. Maybe it was acquiring a full mouthful of adult teeth. A day later Sadow hunted him down to say that the baby's crying disturbed Lolly. "Its crying goes right through her," he told Carson from the front seat of the green car. When Carson suggested they might want to cut short their stay, Sadow told Carson it wasn't an option.

What if they all stayed and stayed? He tried to call Mr. Hayes, but due to the hurricane, phone service was temporarily unavailable.

When Carson couldn't sleep, or wouldn't, he imagined what it was like to be Mr. Hayes, to putter around the property or wait in his little office for the next cast of characters to check in. Instead of sheep, Carson dredged up Cape birds: Grackle, Swallow, Killdeer, Kestrel, Flicker, Blue Jay, Robin, Crow, Kingfisher, Shrike, Mourning Dove. He recalled his dismay at learning it was "mourning" not "morning." When Deidre died, Juliet had been so bereft at losing her that Carson's affair with Deidre felt like a burden he couldn't endure another day. It was why he'd fallen into the meaningless affair with Lisa. He remembered his alarmed relief that she'd succumbed so easily, and then so easily spun him loose when the summer ended. He'd wanted to be found out. He needed to regret an affair that never mattered. Most of all, he needed to lay his heart almost bare. But getting to the place where their hearts were on the table was a reservation neither he nor Juliet could make. Instead, Juliet was out with the car, and he was roaming around the property, pruning the geraniums, poking into sheds, looking under the cabins, inspecting drains as if he were a prospective buyer.

This was how he knew exactly where the shovel was when Jeremy Beek came looking for him. He was cleaning leaves off a wooden canoe that he'd discovered in the trees behind Osprey. Deep circles under Jeremy's eyes testified to the non-vacation the couple was having. When he asked if Hayes Cape Cabins owned a shovel he might borrow, Carson said, sure he had a shovel, and retrieved it from the shed behind the office.

"My wife's good about people. She knew you'd be sensitive to our—ah—situation. Dozer died in his sleep last night. He's been her dog since she was ten. Do you think Mr. Hayes would mind if we buried him here off in the woods?"

Carson longed to be sensitive. Dozer wouldn't take up much space. A bio-degradable dog. Minutes later, he found himself following Jeremy into the woods, far off the path. Every now and then Jeremy stopped to kick at the underbrush, study the ground. Finally he started digging beneath a stand of young oaks and old pines. He was stronger than he looked, and soon, only sweating slightly, he had carved a shallow rectangle in the pine-needle carpet. Dusk was turning the forest floor a dark purple. Carson stood watching because it didn't feel right to leave. The shovel was meant for snow. Finally he told Jeremy, "Here, I'll finish. You go and get—ah—Dozer."

Jeremy wiped his brow on his sleeve; he seemed glad to know he'd have company for the burial, and loped off toward the cabins. Now that night had fallen, Carson was surprised to see they were hidden from view. The dirt was porous and dry, easy to cut away and lift, although Carson's aching shoulders reminded him he hadn't done hard labor for years.

He might have stopped when he had deepened the grave by two more inches, but he didn't. The rhythm had become a mesmerizing physical pull. Suddenly, he shivered against the dark he remembered as a child. He couldn't look up to find the moon, for fear of what else he'd find. He dug and dug and dug. Dirt flew out of the dark into the dark. It was strangely satisfying to rend the earth in preparation for a permanent goodbye. He would have liked to shovel out a portion of Deidre's grave or to begin to fill it in.

Jeremy returned with a flashlight and Dozer wrapped in a blue baby blanket. Standing at the side of the grave, peering in, he seemed taken aback by how deep and wide and long it was—with Carson in it. "Yes, well," Jeremy said. "Dozer will be able to stretch out."

Carson flung his last shovelful of dirt and climbed out; the grave's dark interior had felt ten degrees cooler than the evening's air.

"Ginny insisted I use this blanket," Jeremy said. He knelt down, one knee at a time, and lowered the stiff Dozer into the hole. When he held out his hand for the shovel, Carson surrendered it. Quickly, Jeremy worked to cover the round mound that had been Dozer. "Goodbye, Dozer," he said, tears in his eyes. And in Carson's eyes—Jesus Christ— over a dog he'd only seen a few shit-on-his-shoes times.

When he got back to Osprey, Carson cried full out. He didn't put a name to why. Later that night, no moon, he couldn't sleep. He needed Juliet. Clutching his pillow to his chest, he crept from the too-soft bed in Goldfinch toward Gull. He was stopped by Sadow, who cleared his beard-covered throat and held up a flat, wide palm. "Wait."

Carson threw up his own hands, dropping the pillow. What time was it?

"Whoa, man," Sadow said, his voice low, and, to a terrified Carson, threatening. "You always travel with a pillow?" Sadow picked up the pillow and punched it before handing it back. Carson thanked him and pretended he'd been headed to the office. Following him, Sadow said he and Lolly had some good news for a change. Lolly's brother and sister-in-law were able to get away from their party goods store and would be arriving the next night. He pointed back over his shoulder. "Plover is next door to us. They'll take that one."

Carson fumbled with the office key, threw wide the door, and dumped his pillow on Mr. Hayes's chair. He felt belatedly brave. "I'm sorry. I can't—"

"Wait a minute." Sadow had followed him inside, his gaze roving around the dim messy office. "Something's not normal here." He worked his shoulders in round rolling motions. "That NO VACANCY sign, for one. It went up since we got here. And last I counted you got seven empty cabins."

"Repairs have been scheduled," Carson said.

Sadow scratched his beard. "You never asked for money, a deposit. Never ran our Visa card through the machine."

"If you're unhappy here—" Carson dusted off the credit card machine with his sleeve.

"You don't own this place, do you." It wasn't a question. Sadow slapped the counter. "What were you and Beek up to tonight? I saw you with that shovel."

"Look, why don't you just go dig up the dog. Remember the dog?"

"Dog!" Sadow snorted, and pulled out his cell phone.

Unaccountably, Carson leaned over the counter and knocked it out of his hand.

Tongue between his teeth, Sadow shimmied around the desk and hit a switch on the wall that Carson had never noticed. Lights flooded the cabins with the brightest glow Carson had seen outside of Fenway Park. Of course. Sadow was in construction so he'd know where electricity came from. If he wanted to he could probably turn off the water, put the cabins up on blocks and haul the whole shebang away.

His eye on Sadow, Carson dialed Gull and Tern and pleaded with Juliet and Jeremy to come to the office. Sadow waited, his cell phone back in hand.

Minutes later Juliet appeared in jeans and a sweatshirt. No bra. Hair a burning tangle. "Carson, what is going on?"

Sadow stepped forward to tap her shoulder. "Where's the owner?"

When Juliet said "Florida" Sadow rolled his eyes.

The Beeks arrived running. "What? What?" Jeremy cried, "We saw the lights come on." Ginny's eyes were red and shiny. Oliver was wailing until Lolly appeared at the door and reached for him. He quieted the minute she began murmuring, her cheek against his fuzzy head. "Oh, Lolly, bless you," Ginny Beek said. Jeremy hadn't changed his shirt.

"Tell him," Carson said to Jeremy, "what—who—we buried."

Jeremy's face sagged as he dug into his pocket and pulled out a limp dog collar with two rusted tags. "Dozer," he said, his eyes tearing up. He shrugged toward the glowing woods and Carson. "He helped me bury Dozer."

"Look, Sweetie," Lolly whispered to Sadow as Oliver slept in her arms. "He's sleeping for me."

Juliet's left hand wormed its way into the back of Carson's

waistband and hung there, a weight that left him breathless with longing.

"Dozer. That old dog." Sadow put his cell phone away and patted Oliver's head. All he wanted, he told Juliet, was an extra cabin, and he explained why.

"Why not," Juliet said. "You want Plover?" She gave the key to Lolly who tucked it into Oliver's blanket. Sadow turned off the floods.

"I'm going to bed," Juliet said. One hand was holding back her hair. "Carson. Come to bed."

Once there, her voice cracked. "Oh Carson. You helped Jeremy bury his smelly dog." She started to cry softly.

Carson knew she hated the way she cried, her nose leaking more water than her eyes. Unexpectedly he joined her, snuffling into her hair. Juliet eased her arms out from under his, to lean back, her hands now gripping his trembling arms.

"My sister told me everything," Juliet said. "So, I know."

"Jules…" Carson tried to pull away but she held on tight.

He knew it was true—from his nightmare—that his affair with Deidre was clearly a matter of record, but he hadn't been ready to know it. Even though Juliet's visit to the hospital to deliver his clothes had been so straightforward.

Then Juliet told Carson she wanted him back. "Deidre didn't trust you. But she said I should. So I will, if you tell me to." And so he told her.

They saw fourteen whales on the whale watch. One breached so close to their boat that they could see the barnacles on its teeth. Spray misted the air. The young Beeks from Tern sat in the bow, their baby quieted first by Lolly and then by the boat's engines.

Juliet and Carson stood side by side, hips touching, arms resting on the rail, Juliet's head from time to time dipping to Carson's shoulder. Last night, Juliet had fitted herself around Carson and told him that they would be going on a whale watch with the young Beeks from Tern, the Sadows, and Lolly's sister and brother-in-law who were now staying in Plover. She said it was a trip in memory of Lollypop, the Sadows' daughter—whose cancer, a year ago last fall, burned through her eight-year old body in a race she couldn't win.

Now, as the whaling boat sliced through the water into open seas, Lolly never left the railing. Sadow never left Lolly, who held tight to a Barbie-doll suitcase full of Lollypop's ashes. Lolly's sister and brother-in-law cried as they took videos and photographs and wrote down everyone's address. Lolly's sister had Lolly's Chiclet teeth. When they were out of sight of Provincetown, Lolly let the ashes loose to fall. But the very lightest ash drifted up and over Lolly, over Sadow, and over Carson and Juliet standing next to them at the rail. Carson rubbed the tiny gritty flakes into his cheeks, his lips, touched his finger to his tongue. Juliet's eyes were closed, ash soft on her lashes. Carson took her face in his hands and pulled her to him as he'd done in their cabin in the morning's first light. He hadn't needed to say anything more. Facing her, his fingers in her hair, he'd kneaded her scalp hard, lingering in its slight indentations, releasing the holy oil of grace, then going there.

Acknowledgments

Stories in this collection were originally published in the following:

"Reading in his Wake," *Ploughshares, Pushcart Prize*, W.W. Norton, CD "Love Hurts," Word Theatre

"Fenced In; Fenced Out," *River Styx* (as "Ways to Spend the Night")

"Last Weekend," *Boston Globe Magazine*

"Grief," *Ploughshares, Pushcart Prize*

"Deck," *Five Points*

"The Mystery of Mistakes," *Five Points* (as "Road Trip")

"Trips," *The Normal School*

"Hindsight," *The Kenyon Review*

"Empty Summer Houses," *Pangyrus*

"Prodigal Sister," *Five Points*

"Home Depot," *River Styx*

"Breathe," *Amazon Shorts*, Performed by Word Theatre at SoHo House

"Invention Needs Design," *Mid-American Review*

"Slides," *Green Mountains Review*

"Scenography," *Ploughshares*, (as "Historical Necessity")

"Ways to Spend the Night," *Amazon Shorts*

About the Author

Pamela Painter is the author of three story collections, *Wouldn't You Like to Know, Getting to Know the Weather,* which won the GLCA Award for First Fiction, and *The Long and Short of It.* She is also the co-author of *What If? Writing Exercises for Fiction Writers.* Her stories have appeared in *The Atlantic, Harper's, Kenyon Review, Mid-American Review, Ploughshares,* and *Quick Fiction,* among others, and in numerous anthologies, such as *Sudden Fiction, Flash Fiction, Flash Fiction Forward,* and *MicroFiction.* She has received grants from The Massachusetts Artists Foundation and the National Endowment of the Arts, has won three Pushcart Prizes, and *Agni Review*'s The John Cheever Award for Fiction. Painter's stories have been presented on stage by Word Theatre, Stage Turner, and Wellfleet Harbor Actors Theatre. A recent prize-winning story was recorded on a Norton CD titled "Love Hurts." Painter lives in Boston and teaches in the Writing, Literature and Publishing Program at Emerson College.

CPSIA information can be obtained at www.ICGtesting.com
Printed in the USA
LVOW11s0819161215

466650LV00005B/14/P